C000212701

THE DRAGON'S CHARGE

Tahoe Dragon Mates #4

JESSIE DONOVAN

Mythical Lake Press, LLC

This book is a work of fiction. Names, characters, places, and incidents are either the product of the writer's imagination or are used fictitiously, and any resemblance to actual persons, living or dead, business establishments, events, or locales is entirely coincidental.

The Dragon's Charge
Copyright © 2020 Laura Hoak-Kagey
Mythical Lake Press, LLC
First Print Edition

Cover Art by Laura Hoak-Kagey of Mythical Lake Design
ISBN: 978-1944776206

Want to stay up to date on releases? Please join my newsletter by clicking here to sign-up.

Books in this series:

Tahoe Dragon Mates

The Dragon's Choice (TDM #1)
The Dragon's Need (TDM #2)
The Dragon's Bidder / (TDM #3)
The Dragon's Charge (TDM #4)
The Dragon's Weakness / David & Tiffany (TDM #5 / 2021)

The Dragon's Charge Synopsis

Brad Harper has known that the human bar owner, Tasha Jenkins, is his true mate since he first met her by chance on a night out with friends. However, after his first mate ran off with a human, he's held a grudge and tries to put distance between him and Tasha as best as he can despite working for her. But when both the human female's bar and life are in jeopardy, he has no choice but to protect her. The only question is: Can he resist her?

Tasha Jenkins likes setting goals and achieving them. It's how she was able to establish a successful bar in Reno and be her own boss. However, when some trouble-makers show up and start harassing her clientele, hoping to put her out of business, she struggles with what to do. Then there's a threat to her life, and she finds herself swept into the unknown world of dragon-shifters, where one dragonman in particular seems to both hate her and want to protect her at any cost.

When Tasha has no choice but to stay with Clan StoneRiver, she soon learns more about the dragonman who used to work for her. And just when she thinks she can maybe craft a new path forward, trouble shows up again. Will she be able to get her life back? Or will she find happiness in a place she never thought to look?

NOTE: This is a quick, steamy standalone story about fated mates and sexy dragon-shifters near Lake Tahoe in the USA. You don't have to read all my other dragon books to enjoy this one!

Chapter One

Brad Harper watched the human female named Natasha Jenkins as she smiled and handed a male his final order for the night.

Even though he knew she smiled at almost everyone, he barely resisted digging his nails into his thigh.

His inner dragon—the second personality inside his head—spoke up. *You're the one resisting her, so you have no say. You know she's our true mate.*

Brad had known that fact since the first day he and his friends had walked into Tasha's bar. Of course, who wouldn't notice the female with black hair streaked with blue, warm brown eyes, and brown skin. Skin he wouldn't mind exploring every inch of to better know the curves and valleys of her body.

Not that he would act on his attraction. *And you know why I resist her.*

His inner beast sighed. *So Amber left us for a human male*

over a year ago. That shouldn't make you hate all humans, espe-cially not when it's our fated female.

For a dragon-shifter, a true mate was their best chance at happiness. Not guaranteed, of course, but the odds were usually better. Kissing one would also set off a mate-claim frenzy, basically a nonstop sex marathon that resulted in pregnancy.

Because of that reason, all honorable dragon-shifters had to tread lightly around their true mates, especially if they were human and had no idea of what it all entailed.

He replied to his dragon, *Maybe you can dismiss Amber so easily, but I loved her with everything I had. I'm not about to jump into a true-mate pairing simply because the female showed up. Especially since humans require a lot of work and care, which I don't have the patience for. So stop pushing me.*

Then stop getting jealous when other males smile at her. It's all your own making. She could be smiling at us, if you tried to win her over even a little.

Tasha winked at the tall male at the bar and Brad resisted a growl. *It's not entirely my own making. If David hadn't asked me to take this job as a security guard, I wouldn't have set foot near this place once I'd known about Tasha.*

David Lee was the leader of Clan StoneRiver, the dragon clan situated to the northwest of Lake Tahoe in California. Of course, David was more than just a leader —he was also Brad's friend, one he'd do almost anything for. Which was why he had agreed to the security gig despite everything.

Before his dragon could reply, Brad noticed two human males at one of the bar's back tables stand up, and he watched their movements closely. All evening the pair had given both man and beast an odd tingling sensation, almost as if they were a threat.

And yet they hadn't done anything to merit his throwing their asses out on the street. Yet.

Still, Brad suspected they were part of AHOL—the America for Humans Only League. Most people referred to them as the League, and they were a bunch of crazy fuckers who wanted to drive all dragon-shifters out of the US into other countries. They also targeted businesses friendly to dragon-shifters, with hopes of keeping the two groups separate for good.

Not that any of the stupid assholes realized that dragon-shifters had roamed the earth as long as humans had. While Brad's ancestors were mostly dragon prisoners sent over from Ireland hundreds of years ago—at one time the United States had accepted dragons from other countries in exchange for money and had contained them in prison reservations—many of his clan had always lived in the area, before any of the human European settlers had arrived.

In other words, they had more claim than the vast majority of present-day humans did. Not that the League cared about facts or history. Their hatred guided their every action.

The two males walked casually toward the bar, and Brad moved to the edge of his seat in case he needed to help Tasha. The pair placed an order like any other customer, but Brad didn't move his gaze once. He was used to watching and noticing details. After all, his day job was as a Protector, which was what dragon-shifters called a member of their clan security teams.

Tasha quickly served the humans two beers. One of the males took his and turned away. The other followed suit.

However, just as they took a step away, one of them turned back around and hopped over the bar.

Brad was up in a flash. Even with his supernatural speed, Tasha quickly ducked and then kneed the guy in the dick before Brad could reach her. The attacker dropped to the ground holding himself, and Brad went for the other guy.

Right before he reached the human, the fucker pulled out a gun and aimed it at Tasha. Brad tackled him just as he fired, the shot going wide.

He ignored the screams and chaos to pin the human to the ground, kick away the gun, and quickly check that Tasha was okay.

She met his gaze and nodded shakily. Most people wouldn't notice the minor detail, but Brad had studied the human for months. And she was never shaky.

With a growl, he hauled the male human up and kept the man's hands behind his back.

The human tried to turn his head and spit on Brad before saying, "Get your fucking hands off me, dragon trash."

Brad didn't pay attention to the threat. While laws prevented him from taking out old-style retribution, he could snap the human in half, if he so desired. "Why did you try to shoot a human?"

The other man, who he noticed was now restrained with Tasha's knee on his back, shouted, "Don't say anything."

His gut said there was a quicker way to see if his suspicions about the males were correct. So Brad managed to hold the human male's wrists behind his back with one hand and pushed up the sleeve of the human's arm.

And there it was on his inner wrist, the tattoo all League members had—an eagle clutching a rifle in one claw and an American flag in the other.

Fuck. There'd been an "almost" incident at the bar several weeks ago with a few League members. But since things had been quiet since then, Brad had thought they'd moved on. Especially since no dragon-shifters, apart from him, had set foot inside the bar in recent weeks due to warnings put out by all clan leaders in the area.

Thankfully the human police arrived and took the two men. It was hard for Brad to simply hand over the two assholes since part of his job as a Protector was interrogating enemies.

But the human police dealt with human criminals. So it had been for a long, long time in the US.

His dragon growled. *Which is fucking ridiculous. They tried to kill our mate.*

But they didn't. And us getting thrown in jail would accomplish nothing.

His beast grunted and sulked inside their mind. Brad understood the sentiment but also knew how important it was to follow the human laws, or he could risk the privileges of his entire clan.

Once Tasha gave her statement, as did he, and everyone was cleared out apart from Brad and Tasha, he asked the human abruptly, "Did he say anything to you?"

Tasha twisted her long hair in one hand, which was one of her tells that something was off.

He knew her better than he wanted to.

She sighed and let go of her hair. "Just the usual League bullshit. The cops said they'd keep a closer watch on the place."

Brad wished he could be that optimistic. "Out of all the places in Reno, they randomly picked this one? I doubt it. It's probably related to what happened here a few weeks ago. It made you a target, for sure. So you need to either increase security or close the place for a week or two to let things cool off."

She rolled her eyes. "And you're the boss of me since when?"

He grunted. "No, I'm not your damn boss, and you know it. But I'm trying to keep you alive."

Her brown eyes searched his. "They pull this crap all the time to dragon-friendly businesses, Brad. Usually after one attempt, they fade away for a while. Even you know that. Why should this time be different?"

"Because Duncan Parrish was here weeks ago, that's why. He has friends in powerful places, and we all think he's working with the League, but can't prove it. The male is rich and influential and is used to getting away with anything. So when ADDA pulled rank on him and won, Duncan didn't like it."

ADDA stood for the American Department of Dragon Affairs. They were in charge of all oversight related to dragon-shifters.

One of their employees had been harassed in Tasha's bar by a pair of League members, and afterward, the employee had gotten the dragon clans near Tahoe extra protection. Needless to say, Duncan and his lackeys hadn't liked being thrown out, let alone the new security measures for the Tahoe clans.

Tasha leaned against the counter and shook her head. "I need more than a suspicion to close the bar. This is my entire life, Brad. I won't let a few assholes scare me away. Besides, you're here to help me, and I thought you were the best?"

"I am. But not even I can stop bullets flying at will."

The corner of her mouth ticked up. "I'm sure if there's a way to do it, you'll find it."

A small part of him wanted to tease the human back. But Brad refused to indulge, not wanting to encourage her in any way.

He sensed his dragon about ready to speak up, so he hurriedly said to Tasha, "Joking around won't change anything. You need to close the bar for a little while, period."

She raised her brows. "So they can target me at home? Hiding away won't help me, if they're truly determined."

The human was right. However, there was one place the League members would never set foot—Clan Stone-River. For all their talk about hating dragons and wanting to get rid of them, they were cowards when it truly came down to it. Visiting dragon clans wasn't part of their usual actions. Especially with ADDA monitoring the clans more than before.

Not that he was going to suggest for Tasha to come live on his clan, though. No, he'd make sure her house was safe and then set up a constant watch. That might be a solution the human could live with.

As she continued to stare at him, clearly waiting for an answer, Brad motioned toward the back door. "Then let me make sure you get home safe, at least. We'll talk more about this tomorrow."

"This isn't your bar, Brad. And it's not your decision to make."

Maybe he should be nicer to Tasha, given everything that had happened, but even if he had no intention of claiming his true mate, he'd sure as hell protect her. Which meant being truthful. "I know this is your place, Tasha. But you hired me to be security, and I'm not going to push aside my duty because you don't like how I do my job."

As she studied him, he wondered if he'd have to lay out even more facts to get her out the door. But she finally sighed and headed toward the back area. "Fine, I'll go home for now. If you weren't so damn good at your job, I'd be tempted to fire you."

He grunted in response as his inner dragon spoke up again. *She has noticed us. That's good, very good. Maybe with time, you'll tell her the truth.*

Not ready to rehash the same argument, he ignored his beast and instead ensured the coast was clear to see Tasha out.

Just as they reached her car parked behind the building, he noticed all four tires were flat. There was also a piece of folded paper stuck under her windshield.

As his dragon growled in warning, Brad ordered, "Stay here but stay alert. Something's wrong."

The human female nodded, clearly still surprised at the slashed tires. Brad plucked up the note, opened it, and read, "This is your final warning. Shun all dragons or face the consequences."

There was no signature, but just a stamp at the bottom of the note with the League's logo.

He stormed up to Natasha, knowing the note had changed everything.

She would have to come home to his clan after all. Which meant finding new ways to stay away from her while also protecting her.

Brad handed her the note, and once she finished reading it, he stated, "You're coming home with me tonight to StoneRiver. Don't argue, either. Because none of your arguments are worth your life."

He gestured toward his car farther down the street and waited to see if Tasha would agree or if he'd have to act the part of barbaric dragon-shifter and carry her to his vehicle.

Not because she was his true mate and his dragon was growling about her safety. No, Brad convinced himself it was because she'd hired him to protect her, and he prided himself on being the best. Nothing more.

TASHA JENKINS WASN'T STUBBORN for the sake of it. Her perseverance had helped her over the years to achieve a lot of her goals. It was how she'd come to own a successful bar in Reno, one that had become even more profitable when she'd finally opened her doors to dragon-shifters.

So when some assholes had tried to scare her, she'd tried to brush it off. It wasn't the first fight or time a man had tried to harm her. When people drank too much, sometimes shit happened.

But as she stared at the note in her hands about a final warning, and then glanced at her slashed tires, she knew that this was more than an idle threat to scare her. The crazy AHOL bastards might actually try to kill her.

It seemed that when she'd stood by the ADDA employee Ashley Swift and her dragonman date over a month ago, she'd made some dangerous enemies.

Since the jurisdictions were all messed up when human and dragon worlds collided, like they did with the League, she didn't have faith the police would take it all seriously despite their promises. They could entirely brush it off as ADDA's responsibility and look the other way.

In other words, she needed the help of dragon-shifters if she was to survive.

So when Brad stated she was going home to his clan for the night, she knew it was the only option. So she nodded. "For tonight. But I plan on figuring this out, Brad. I won't give up my bar this easily."

He grunted, took her hand, and guided her down the street.

Tasha tried to ignore how warm and large his hand was around hers. In her experience, most dragonmen were sexy, muscled, and had some sort of draw that most human women—and quite a few men—had a hard time resisting.

Not only was she determined to avoid being distracted by any man—dragon or otherwise—she knew Brad Harper didn't like her much. He only worked at her bar as a favor to his clan leader, and most days he ignored her unless a security threat cropped up.

The fact he had to protect her and watch out for her was probably nothing more than a nuisance. He most definitely wasn't holding her hand because he wanted to. No, he wanted to ensure she didn't change her mind.

Which showed just how little he knew her. Because once Tasha made up her mind, she stuck to it until circumstances required her to take another look.

They finally reached his small, blue car, and Brad motioned for her to stay put again. She watched as he inspected the engine and the undercarriage. It was strange seeing him do anything but sit in a corner and survey the room with his piercing blue eyes, like he did most nights at her bar.

And she most definitely wasn't going to notice how broad his shoulders were, or how quickly he moved without making a sound.

For the first time since initially hiring him, Tasha wondered more about his life on StoneRiver. And not just because she was possibly entrusting her life to him right now, either.

Brad jumped to his feet and gestured toward the passenger side. "Get in."

While she didn't normally like taking orders, she was eager to get under the protection of the dragon-shifters for the night. So, she slid into the seat. However, once they were both inside the car, she asked, "What can you do in one night to help me?"

He pulled out onto the street. "It'll give us time to make a plan."

She noticed the "us" part of his statement. "I'm grateful for your help earlier, I really am. But I'm not sure I follow how you and your clan can help me once I'm no longer on StoneRiver."

He gripped the steering wheel tighter. "League activity has increased in recent months. Given what we've heard on my clan, they're starting to target humans, too. I had hoped I was wrong, but after tonight, the whole situation is a lot more serious than you think, Tasha." He finally glanced at her. "I'm not being dramatic when I say your life might be changing forever in the next few days."

She searched his gaze, noting how his pupils flashed between round and slitted, revealing his inner dragon's presence. Maybe to some, the sight would be weird. But she'd grown used to flashing dragon eyes. So she merely replied, "That's vague as hell, Brad."

He shook his head. "I can't say anything else until we talk with my clan leader. David will have a better idea of how to handle ADDA than me."

"If you're going to rely on ADDA, then let me call Ashley. She said to call her anytime."

"And you might have to. But let's wait and see if the men from tonight are charged or not. That will tell us a lot about if the police will help or look the other way."

She studied him once more, noting his strong jaw and

slightly crooked nose before asking slowly, "What do you mean 'if' they are charged? I know the police can be wishy-washy when it comes to dragon-related crimes, but they attacked a human. There's no disputing it."

He growled. "We're still gathering proof, but we think some of the local police are League sympathizers."

Shit. If that were true, then the situation had gone from a little jarring to downright dangerous.

And for the first time in over a decade, Tasha wasn't sure of what to do.

Brad's voice interrupted her thoughts. "Don't worry, even if the police give up on you, we won't. David promised to help look after your bar for reasons not even I understand. But just know that he's an honorable male and will see it through."

While never confirmed, Tasha suspected it had something to do with her aunt and someone from StoneRiver. She'd heard rumors about how her aunt had tried to run away with a StoneRiver dragon-shifter but had been caught and moved across the country. For all she knew, a promise had been made or something. Her aunt had passed before Tasha could ever ask her about it all.

Regardless, she would take StoneRiver's help for now. It'd give Tasha time to talk with Ashley Swift, who still worked for ADDA, and a few other people she trusted. Maybe she could come up with a solution that meant she could still run her bar and sleep in her own bed without constantly looking over her shoulder for another bullet.

Because she didn't want to listen to the tiny voice inside her head, the one saying she might have to sell her bar and start over somewhere else. Tasha had worked too hard for too long to give up on her business.

There had to be a solution, there just had to.

But as Brad drove them to StoneRiver, exhaustion finally won the battle over her racing thoughts, and she fell asleep.

Chapter Two

Brad being stuck in a car for nearly two hours with Tasha was pure hell. And not just because normally he'd park at the edge of the forest, shift into his dragon form, and quickly fly the rest of the way home instead of taking the long drive.

No, it was hell because his dragon kept mentioning her heat, or how her lips parted as she slept, or how nice it was to be surrounded by her scent.

All things Brad didn't want to notice but couldn't help doing so in such a confined space.

Gripping the steering wheel tighter, he tried to focus on what could be done about Tasha's bar instead of the fact his true mate slept in the seat next to him. The sooner he figured out that problem, the sooner he could put distance back between them again.

His dragon yawned. *Aren't you getting tired of denying your attraction yet? You notice her as much as I do. And if you push her away for good, you know you'll regret it.*

Pushing her away will mean a hell of a lot fewer problems.

So you'd rather the League target her than be around her?

I didn't say that.

His inner beast sighed. *You make no sense whatsoever. Talk to me again once you figure it all out.*

As silence fell inside his mind, it took every iota of strength Brad possessed to keep his eyes on the road and ignore the sleeping female.

His dragon was right—she smelled so damn good. He imagined waking up next to her, with his nose at her neck, and it made his cock stir.

Fuck. He was supposed to resist her. Humans equaled trouble in his book. Besides, he'd loved Amber.

He nearly blinked. Brad had used the past tense, which he'd never done when thinking of her before.

Had he finally gotten over Amber? He'd been so fucking in love with her and had been about to propose when she'd fled in the middle of the night. No one had known she was gone until the next day, not even him.

His beast whispered, *Amber is no longer here. But Tasha is right there.*

He dared a glance at the human's sleeping face. She leaned against the window, her hair lying against her cheek. He itched to touch the blue streaks she had in it, curious as to why she constantly changed the color there.

What am I doing? He most definitely didn't need the headache of a true mate on his plate. Dancing around her, never kissing her until she was ready, would distract him from his work, both for the clan and to keep her safe. After all, a dead Tasha was of no use to anyone.

His dragon said smugly, *But you're starting to think it's worth trying with her. Deny it all you want, but you can't lie to me.*

Damn his dragon and his meddling.

But then they reached the main entrance to StoneRiver. Brad ignored his beast to pull up to the intercom and keypad unit situated several feet away from the twelve-foot-high metal gates. While height was nothing to a dragon-shifter who could fly over them, the spikes on top helped to keep human enemies or the dragon groupies out.

Brad typed in the correct code, and the gates swung inward. When he finally pulled in front of the main security building, he sent a text message to David to meet them, also letting his leader know about the further threats. Since he'd called his leader while the police had been talking to Tasha earlier, David knew mostly what was going on already.

A reply pinged back straight away from David, saying he'd be there soon. Tucking his phone into his pocket, Brad turned slightly toward Tasha.

She was still asleep. He had no idea if she was a heavy sleeper or if on some level, she trusted him to protect her.

His dragon said, *I think it's the latter.*

Not wanting to give his dragon hope in the true mate department, Brad reached over and lightly brushed Tasha's arm. She moved a little but didn't wake up.

So he touched a finger to her jaw, daring to stroke her warm, soft skin.

Electricity raced up his arm and ended between his legs. Damn, if touching her with just his fingers was this dangerous, he needed to be careful. If she ever crashed into him, Brad might not be able to resist her.

Good. Then I'll have to make that happen, his dragon stated.

He continued brushing Tasha's cheek until she finally blinked her eyelids open. Even in the almost darkness, he loved the deep brown color of her eyes. She finally glanced out the window—the front of the security building had lights, so her human eyesight could see it—and then asked, "Are we on StoneRiver?"

"Yes. Now, come on. My clan leader is coming to meet us."

She scrunched up her nose. "Can't I use the bathroom first? After all, wild hair and dried drool won't make a very good impression, and I should be halfway presentable with a dragon clan leader."

His lips twitched. "You look fine."

She raised an eyebrow. "I could be covered in mud and feathers and a man would still say I look fine. Sorry, but your words aren't very reassuring."

He chuckled and nearly did a double take. He wasn't one to laugh easily, and here the human had made him do it.

His dragon whispered, *Give her a chance.*

Not ready to deal with that comment, he opened his door. "Come on. The sooner we talk with David, the sooner we can find you a place to sleep for the night."

Without waiting for her reply, he exited the car and stood in front of it. Thankfully Tasha followed suit, and he guided her inside the security building. With any luck, he'd be free of the human female's intoxicating presence soon enough and he could finally clear his head.

TASHA FOLLOWED Brad inside a several-story building she couldn't really make out in the almost darkness. So much for gawking at the inside grounds of Clan StoneRiver for the first time. Her curiosity would just have to wait until morning.

Inside the building, the halls looked like many other hallways she'd seen—tiled floors and neutral-colored walls that she could only describe as light brown-ish. It wasn't exactly what she'd imagined her first impression of a dragon clan would be. It was almost…normal. For all the rumors and tales about the dragons, they might be a lot more like humans than most people believed.

Serving dragon-shifters at her bar had definitely opened her eyes to how similar they were to humans in public. But she still imagined something a little more special when it came to their home turf.

Brad guided her into a room—another nondescript place with a table and chairs—and motioned toward one of the seats. He said, "David will be here soon. Sit down and I'll get you some water."

She nodded and Brad exited the room. Tasha tapped her feet as she waited, trying not to let her mind run wild.

After all, she might, *just might*, have a hateful group bent on driving all dragons out of the country targeting her. She was safe for the time being, but that could change at any moment. Especially if the police ended up being sympathetic to the League guys who'd tried to shoot her.

And tough as she may be, Tasha wasn't stupid. She wouldn't be able to fend off the League on her own if they were indeed outside the law. She needed help, plain and simple. And not just any kind of help, but from the dragon-shifters.

However, she had no idea how—or if—the StoneRiver dragons would be willing to help her. And if they did offer to do so, there had to be a price. No one would risk so much for free, at least in her experience.

The door opened, revealing Brad's tall, broad-shouldered figure. She barely noted how much more at ease he seemed here than at her bar when another man entered behind him. The man with short, black hair, golden skin, and assessing brown eyes was no stranger. She'd met him before—StoneRiver's clan leader, David Lee.

David smiled at her and sat opposite. Brad took the seat next to her.

Before she could say anything, David spoke up. "It seems you being nice to us has backfired spectacularly. Believe me when I say that I never intended for this all to happen."

She shrugged one shoulder. "I know that. You can't control assholes and their actions."

David snorted. "True. But you opened your bar as a favor to me and Ashley Swift. And while I can't speak for Ashley, I can for me. And now that you're in trouble, you're under my protection."

She frowned. "But only for as long as I stay here. You know as well as I do that dragon-shifters can't stay full-time in Reno. I'll just have to hire some human security guards."

Brad grunted. "That won't be enough."

She had a feeling he was right. But for some reason, she wanted to push back against him. Almost as if she didn't do it now, she might regret it later. "How do you know that? The League are human, so other humans should be able to stop them."

David jumped in. "Except that in recent months, the League has been glorifying self-sacrifice. And that is a huge fucking problem for all of us."

She resisted blinking at the statement. It was the first she'd heard of it. "What the hell are you talking about?"

David sighed. "Someone is trying to drive up the hatred of dragon-shifters again. And one surefire way to do it is to make sacrificing themselves for the cause as some fucking brave, patriotic act. Something like cleansing the US of dragons will make the humans the strongest, the richest, insert whatever you like here in the world. In their line of thinking, dragon-shifters only hold them back or drag them down."

She blinked. "How in the hell are dragons holding people back?"

David replied, "They're not. But most League members are looking for someone to blame for their problems, troubles, or whatever is wrong in their lives. And so dragons are those targets. They dismissed the League down in Florida, and now it's chaotic there. I hope we can keep the same thing from happening here, but I'm still working on how to do that exactly."

Tasha looked from David to Brad and back again.

"Why haven't I heard anything about this? I would think that a crazy hate group willing to commit suicide to kill a dragon would make the news."

David shook his head. "ADDA is trying to keep it quiet, as are the officials of the human cities in Florida. I doubt even the other Tahoe clans know what's going on."

Great. So rather than a minor pain in the ass, the League idiots could possibly be out to sacrifice themselves for the cause. In that case, burning down her bar or using an explosive wouldn't be out of the question.

Tasha was used to isolating a problem, figuring out the best solution, and bouncing back up again. However, she might not be able to follow the same strategy this time. Death was pretty permanent, and no amount of security guards could protect her from the crazies.

For the first time in her life, Tasha was glad her parents were no longer alive because if they were, then they'd become targets, too.

Taking a deep breath, she met David's eyes again. "So then, what are my options?"

He nodded. "I like your levelheadedness, Tasha. I'm not sure many humans would be as strong as you."

She waved a hand in dismissal. "I've had to face more challenges than most to get to where I am. It's nothing new." She leaned forward. "So don't keep me waiting, David. What can be done?"

David replied, "The only way to truly protect you is to keep you on StoneRiver. I know Clan PineRock has been having some problems with the League, too, thanks to information from Ashley Swift. If I reach out to them, we can work together to maybe figure out a solution."

She frowned. "But I can't stay on StoneRiver forever. I have a life, my bar, my house, and my friends."

David smiled sadly. "I know it won't be easy, but you'll have to give them up. At least for a little while. There is a way for you to stay on StoneRiver, but I need you to have an open mind about it."

Okay, that didn't sound very promising. "What is it?" she asked slowly.

David shrugged. "You can mate a dragon-shifter. Eventually you can divorce him or her—I don't know your preference—but the mating will allow you to stay here legally for as long as you like."

She blinked and tried to process what David had just said. "You want me to marry, er mate, a dragon-shifter? What will you do, just pick some poor guy at random?"

Brad grunted. "It'll be me."

She whipped her head around, her usual filter forgotten. "But you can't stand me."

He cleared his throat. "That's not exactly true."

Feeling lost, she glanced at David and back to Brad. If she was to get any true answers, she was going to be blunt. "But you always walk away from me as quickly as possible, barely mutter a sentence at me a day, and always glare at me."

"There's a reason for all that."

She stared him down. "Which is?"

For the first time ever, Brad shifted in his seat and looked uncomfortable.

It seemed her usually unflappable part-time security guard wasn't as devoid of emotion as he usually portrayed.

David's voice filled the room. "Either tell her, Brad, or I will. She deserves to know before committing to anything."

Okay, David's words made Tasha a little leery of Brad's secret.

Still, she wasn't going to just brush it aside or be afraid of the truth. "Tell me, Brad. Whatever it is, I'm sure I can handle it. I mean, someone tried to shoot me a few hours ago. It can't be that bad."

He sat up straight and cleared his throat. "Well, that depends on how you look at it. You're my true mate, Tasha. That's why I've kept my distance."

"True mate?" she echoed, trying to remember what she could about the phrase. "Isn't that like some fated-bride scenario or something?"

Brad nodded. "Yes, my inner dragon recognizes you as our best chance at happiness."

Okay, that was even more fantasy-like than she'd imagined. Especially since Tasha didn't believe in fate in the first place. Still, if Brad believed it, then he'd been pretty damn good at keeping it a secret. She blurted, "Then why have you tried so hard to stay away from me?"

He muttered, "It's complicated."

Tasha rolled her eyes. "More complicated than being a target of some sort of domestic terrorist group? One, whom I might add, is this close to killing you?"

Brad grunted. "Maybe."

She growled in frustration. "For something this important, you're going to stick to a nonanswer?"

David jumped in before Brad could reply. "It's late,

and we all should rest before picking up this conversation in the morning. ADDA won't notice you staying here a day—you could be looking for another part-time security guard, for all they know—which gives us time to figure this all out."

She frowned. "You say that as if it's decided that I'll stay here."

"There's not really another choice, Tasha. Take the night to think about it and then we'll talk further." David stood. "Brad's sister has an extra room and you can stay there. Megan is a lot friendlier than her brother, so don't worry about a warm welcome."

If she were to guess, David wanted her to warm up to Brad through his sister. But little did he know that until she had an honest conversation with Brad, she wasn't going to consider the decision to marry him, or whatever the dragons called it, her only option.

She stood. "Okay, then let's go so I can get some sleep. But I hope we can snag some food on the way since I haven't eaten yet."

Brad's deep voice came from behind her. "I'll ensure you have something to eat. Come on."

"I'll see you in the morning, Tasha," David stated. "Good night."

Something about the tone of his voice told her there was no arguing the point. Everything would have to wait until morning.

And she felt like she should obey, which was weird. It must be yet more dragon-shifter magic, of a sort.

So she merely followed Brad out of the room and down the same corridor. Only once they were outside did she stop in her tracks. When Brad finally turned toward her, she said, "I can't wait until morning to hear this answer of yours, Brad. Why've you done your damnedest to make me think you hate me?"

As she watched his pupils flash in the dim light, she wondered what his inner dragon was saying.

But since she couldn't read minds, Tasha waited for the man to answer.

BRAD KNEW he should've been prepared for Tasha's question. Ever since he'd run into David in the hall and his clan leader had mentioned how mating Tasha was the best course of action, he'd dreaded having to explain everything.

And now here she was, his fated female, wanting answers.

His dragon huffed. *It's because even you're realizing how stupid your reasons sound.*

Not entirely true. I don't reveal everything about myself to most people.

But she's our true mate, one that we're about to mate officially. She should know the truth.

Brad didn't have it in him to argue that Tasha hadn't said yes to the mating yet.

Instead, he studied the human female in the dim light, his dragon-shifter eyesight allowing him to see her as clearly as in bright daylight.

Her brows were pinched a little as she stared at him. Even though he was so much taller, and stronger, and

could shift into a mighty dragon, she didn't show a bit of
fear. Maybe she was a little afraid, but if so, he couldn't
tell.

For a human, she was incredibly strong.

Which, damn it, made him want to tell her more
than he should.

Brad finally replied, "The reason I tried to brush you
off all the time is because when humans and dragon-
shifters get involved, things get complicated. If nothing
else, you should know that from what happened with
Ashley and Wes Dalton."

Wes was the clan leader of PineRock, another dragon
clan in the greater Tahoe area. Brad didn't know him
well, but the two clans hadn't been actual enemies in a
long, long time. And not attacking or threatening Stone-
River made the dragon leader somewhat okay in his
book.

Tasha nodded. "Yes, I know that, but not just from
what happened to Wes and Ashley, either. Remember
that when a place opens its doors to dragons, we have to
memorize a set of laws and take a test."

He growled, "The laws are the fucking problem."

She tilted her head. "While I can see that point of
view, I think there's more to it. Something you aren't
telling me."

His dragon stood up tall inside his mind. *She's really
preceptive.*

*Are you surprised? Nothing happens in her bar that she doesn't
know about.*

Brad could brush it off and tell her to wait until
morning, as David had said.

But now that his fate was almost assuredly tied to hers —Tasha was smart and would see how mating him was the only way StoneRiver could protect her for the foreseeable future—Brad decided fuck it. He'd be honest and see how she reacted. "Humans cause trouble. One stole my ex from me. They ran away in the middle of the night, and I have no idea what happened to her. She could've fucking died for all we know. She should've waited and at least consulted the clan leader. But no, she didn't. And I'm sure the human was the reason she didn't."

And there was his truth. He'd been hurt by her betrayal, of course he'd been. But the days, weeks, and months of wondering whether Amber was still alive or not had been the worst part.

No doubt the human had convinced her to run. And a dragon-shifter on the run became a target of ADDA, the League, and possibly rival clans. The four Tahoe clans weren't exactly friendly with one another, but they at least each minded their own damn business and stayed out of trouble.

However, in some parts of the country, a foreign dragon-shifter entering their territory marked them as enemy number one. True, it was against the law to murder, but some dragon clans did a lot of things on the sly, uncaring about modern-day laws.

His dragon said softly, *Amber would've known all that and still taken the risk. Maybe there was a reason she ran, we don't know.*

Tasha's voice interrupted Brad's reply to his dragon. "Ashley tells me all the time that I shouldn't base my opinion on the actions of one dragon-shifter. Sure, the bastard ones end up in the news and then make everyone think you're all murderers or thieves, or 'insert criminal type here.' But it works both ways, Brad. Maybe that human guy your ex ran off with made a rash decision, or was persuasive. However, it could've been a joint decision. Regardless, basing your opinion on all humans because one stole your girlfriend is a little stupid, in my opinion."

He blinked. "Did you just call me stupid?"

She bobbed her head. "A little, yes. Oh, you're really good at spotting troublemakers or noticing people about to act like idiots in the bar. I've never had a security guard as good as you. But in this one instance, regarding your opinion on humans? Yes, you're an idiot."

His dragon laughed. *I like her even more, if that's possible.*

Considering she's our true mate, I don't think so.

But he had to give it to Tasha—she was right. Deep down, he knew she was. However, admitting it wasn't the easiest thing. Especially since that belief had kept him together for the months after Amber had left, giving him someone to hate for his loss.

His dragon spoke up. *It's been a long time now. Maybe you should be more open-minded. Even knowing the risks, Tasha opened her bar to our kind. She, at the very least, deserves a chance.*

Not wanting to answer his beast, Brad grunted. "Maybe I am biased. But it's much more than my past that made me try to avoid you, Tasha. My dragon noticing how you're my true mate makes everything complicated. Imagine being constantly drawn to someone despite what you're feeling. And then if you accidentally kiss them, it starts off a sex marathon that only ends in pregnancy. So I have more than one reason for being cautious. I was protecting us both."

She raised her eyebrows. "What century is this? I can —and have made—many of my own decisions, Brad Harper. Did you never think to share this with me and see what I say about it?"

His dragon muttered, *I suggested that all the damn time.*

Ignoring his beast, he replied, "If I had told you the truth, then what? Would you have instantly given up everything to move to a dragon clan? Mating a dragon-shifter means living with them on their clan. There's no way around that in the US. And despite what you may think of me, I know how much your bar means to you. It's hard enough opening your own business, but then to have it be profitable and stay that way? It's a big fucking deal."

Her furrowed brows eased a fraction. "Of course it's important to me. And who knows how I would've reacted. But you still should've told me, especially given the whole sex marathon possibility."

As Tasha stood in the mostly darkness, the light wind blowing her hair to the side, her eyes strong and deter-mined, he forgot about his past for a second. Tasha Jenkins was fucking beautiful, strong, and would never cower before anyone.

She had the heart of a warrior, or better yet, a dragon-shifter.

His dragon spoke up. *And she could be ours for more than a fake mating, too. If you tried to win her, even just a little.*

Brad had spent so much time trying to avoid the

human female, not wanting to betray his former love and his own stubborn ass. He was a Protector after all, and tried to be as honorable, strong, and loyal as he should be.

However, maybe he'd taken his loyalty to his former love, Amber, too far and had instead used it as a shield.

His beast snorted. *And now look who's becoming all soft and poetic.*

He cleared his throat. "So now you know the truth. What will you do?"

Tasha shrugged. "That I don't know just yet. While our little chat has helped me understand you better, I'm not sure one conversation will convince me to give up my entire life."

He wanted to force her to stay so he could protect her. But he tamped down his urges and said, "I hate to say it, but if you don't agree to David's plan, you may end up doing so anyway. And possibly more permanently."

She didn't so much as bat an eyelash at his hint of being killed. "Maybe. But I need some time to think. Where's your sister's place? We can talk more in the morning, once I sort through some things."

Ten minutes ago, Brad would've jumped at the chance to get rid of her.

And now?

Well, now, he was all confused about what to do with his fated female.

His dragon spoke up. *Spending the night apart will help both sides.*

And now you're the rational one?

Information is powerful, and it may be enough to sway her. So yes, I can wait a few hours to talk more with her, especially considering how you've avoided her as much as possible for months.

Damn dragon giving him whiplash with his moods.

With a grunt, Brad gestured toward the right. "This way. I'm sure David called Megan, so she should be awake and ready for us."

And far quicker than he liked, Brad handed over Tasha's care to his sister and headed toward his own house. It was going to be a long fucking night, that was for sure. Especially since he wasn't entirely sure what he wanted to do with Tasha just yet.

His beast whispered, *Oh, you know. But I'll give you the night to realize it yourself.*

With that, his dragon curled up inside his mind and went to sleep. And Brad spent the next few hours imagining life with or without Tasha, trying to figure it all out.

Chapter Three

The next morning, as Tasha sat across from the pale, blue-eyed form of Megan Lee, she sipped her coffee and noted the activity in the kitchen.

Megan's mate, Justin Lee, was helping to feed their youngest child. While the man seemed nice enough, it hadn't taken Tasha long to learn he was David Lee's cousin. So her staying with Megan wasn't a spur-of-the-moment decision. No, not only was she staying with Brad's sister, but another person closely tied to the clan's security, too.

Not that she had gotten any sort of weird vibes from either of them. Justin was firm with the children when needed, but clearly doted on them as he helped serve up breakfast.

Megan was both friendly and chatty, but Tasha suspected the woman didn't miss a thing that happened in her house.

After all, Tasha was just as perceptive, and it often took a perceptive person to recognize another one.

As Tasha sipped her coffee, Megan said, "I've been beating around the bush all morning. So tell me—what are you going to do?"

Justin shook his head. "Can't she eat in peace?"

Megan tsked. "It's not an unreasonable question for me to ask. Better she figures out the answer now than when she talks with David, right?"

Tasha cleared her throat and all eyes—including those of the three children aged five and under—moved to her. Tasha placed her mug down and asked, "Is this how it works on dragon clans, then? Everyone keeps deciding or trying to convince someone of what's best for everyone else without asking them?"

Justin grinned. "Well, I can't speak for all clans, but it works that way here."

Great. So everyone would always be in her business.

Maybe if she knew them better, she wouldn't mind. But she'd had to be super careful about sharing any sort of personal information whenever working at the bar. After all, she didn't want a drunk person showing up at her place and serenading her window. Or worse, someone trying to break into her house and do who knows what.

Megan spoke before Tasha could. "But it's not all bad here. Some people do manage to keep to themselves. After all, my brother is an extremely private person for StoneRiver. But even if he doesn't talk about it, I can tell he's still brooding about that female that left him."

"Megan," Justin said slowly as a warning. The pair shared some sort of nonverbal conversation, which was only interrupted by the five-year-old, who slipped out of his chair and ran over to Tasha. He poked her arm and smiled. "You're pretty. Be my mate?"

At the little boy's sweet brown eyes and shy smile, Tasha forgot about meddling dragon-shifters and turned toward Andrew. "I think I'm too old for you, Andy. But someday you'll find your own mate."

Andrew sighed and hung his head. "Okay."

The complete dejection from the little boy did something to Tasha's heart. She touched his shoulder and he looked up at her again. "We can be friends, though. Is that okay?"

And just like that, his eyes lit up. "My first human friend."

His words reminded Tasha of something she wanted to ask Megan. However, she first ruffled the boy's brown hair and replied, "That's right. I'll gladly be your first human friend. Now, why don't you finish your breakfast? I need to talk with your mom."

Megan said softly yet sternly, "She's right, Andy. Finish your fruit, like you promised you would. And no hiding it under the table like yesterday."

"Okay, Mom," Andrew said dramatically and trudged to the other side of the table, taking absolutely as long as possible to get there.

It took everything she had not to laugh at the theatrics.

She hadn't spent much time around children for

years, but Megan and Justin's kids seemed like a good group to get reacquainted with them again.

Although seeing two dragon-shifters having breakfast with their three kids made her wonder if this was what it would be like with her own family. Provided she agreed to the mating with Brad, of course. And if it went well, then agreed to the sex-marathon deal that would supposedly guarantee a baby at the end.

Tasha hadn't spent a lot of time thinking about what she wanted in the relationship and family department. Her bar had been everything.

But now, she had little choice but to wonder about what she truly wanted. Being targeted by a crazy terrorist group sort of put things in perspective. Did she want to give up her bar? Of course not. But maybe she wanted more in her life now, on top of owning a successful business.

Megan's voice brought Tasha back to the present. "What did you want to talk to me about?"

She looked back at Megan's smiling face. Tasha's gut said the woman could be a good ally to have if she stayed on StoneRiver.

Although that was still a big if to staying. "Are there any other humans living on StoneRiver? Brad has never exactly been chatty, and he's the only real dragon-shifter I've known for more than an hour or two here and there. Dragon customers tend to keep their clan life pretty secret."

Megan answered, "Yeah, I imagine they would. After all, the League is why you're here, right? We have to worry about them, and others like them, all the time."

Tasha nodded—the daily lives of dragon-shifters were becoming more real to her—and Megan continued, "But no, as of right now, there aren't any other humans. Clan PineRock has at least three humans living with them, although there's talk of some sibling of the human male —what was his name? Oh, that's right, Ryan Ford—petitioning to move there, too."

Since Tasha didn't keep track of dragon mates—it wasn't as if many of her customers had revealed them to her at the bar anyway—she had no idea who Megan was talking about. So instead, she focused on StoneRiver. "So I would be the only human living here then."

Megan smiled sadly and said, "Yes, at least for the moment. Although now that Ashley has mated a dragon-shifter—which gives her even more reason to push for humans to be allowed to mate a dragon if they want—I suspect it'll change soon."

It seemed everyone knew Ashely Swift. Tasha really needed to reach out to her ASAP and get some advice. She'd been too tired the night before to make the call, and she wasn't about to call her at the ass-crack of dawn.

As Tasha pondered being the only human surrounded entirely by dragon-shifters, the doorbell echoed inside the house. Megan went to answer it and came back with her brother right behind her.

Brad found her gaze and grunted. "Good morning."

The words were simple, but as she held his blue-eyed gaze, a small tingle rushed through her body.

She'd allowed herself to think of Brad as more than just her employee last night. And as a result, the hour or two of sleep she'd finally nabbed had been filled with fantasies, such as him stripping her slowly before kissing her. Not knowing what a mate-claim frenzy entailed—she'd learned the actual name of the sex marathon—her dreams had also been full of hot, often rough sex.

Had he dreamt the same thing over the night? Or had his hatred of humans been front and center?

Brad's pupils flashed repeatedly, but he never looked away.

And neither did she.

ON THE WALK to his sister's house, Brad had managed to pack away all his emotions like he normally did, bracing himself to face Tasha and her mesmerizing eyes.

But then she'd had to go and stare at him as if she could lick him from head to toe and still not get enough, shattering most of his hard work.

If her heated gaze hadn't been enough, he'd never forget the scent of his true mate's arousal. She saw him as more than her security guard now. Which meant that between last night and this morning, her view about him had shifted.

His dragon sighed. *Which most dragon-shifters would take as a sign to pursue. But you're still going to resist, aren't you? Because her scent doesn't have to be a one-time memory.*

While Brad was no longer outright arguing with his beast about Tasha, he still hadn't convinced his human half that mating the human—and making it a true mating—was a good idea. *Remember our deal.*

I know, I know. I need to let you have some time to talk with her and then with David before I badger you again.

His sister's voice snapped Brad out of the moment. "Well, good to see your manners are as bad as ever, Brad."

Since he knew Megan would go on to annoy him like any little sister would if he didn't brush past her comment, he merely grunted.

His oldest nephew, Andrew, stood up in his seat, fork in the air. The blueberry on one of the fork prongs nearly came off in the process. "Hi, Uncle Brad. I eat my fruit. Then I get a hug."

His two nephews and niece were his weakness when it came to remaining stoic. He smiled slightly at Andrew. "Fruit is good for you. If you don't eat enough, your teeth can fall out."

Andrew poked one of his little front teeth. "Fall out?"

"Yes. There's some good stuff in fruit and some other foods that help keep them strong and in your mouth."

Tasha's amused voice replied, "Educating the kids about scurvy is admirable, if not a little weird."

Andrew asked, "What's skirt-vee?"

He gestured for Tasha to explain. His human didn't bat an eyelash and turned toward the boy. "Scurvy. If you don't get enough of something called vitamin C, your teeth can fall out." She lowered her voice. "Although most people do okay these days. It was many, many years ago that people didn't have enough fruits and veggies and had to worry about it. So make sure to eat your fruit and vegetables—and brush your teeth, too— and your teeth should be okay."

Andrew squinted at the blueberry on his fork. "Eat all of them?"

Tasha nodded. "As many as you can. Well, the parts your mom and dad give you in your meals, anyway. If you ate all the fruits and veggies in the world, you might explode. You know, BOOM."

Tasha threw her hands out and Andrew giggled.

In that moment, Brad realized Tasha would be a great mother.

So not only was she smart about business and sexy as hell, she was good with kids, too.

For most dragon-shifters, that was it—they'd try their damnedest to win over such a person.

Brad wasn't most people, though. He'd jumped into a relationship with everything he'd had and had been abandoned without more than a few words on a page.

His dragon sighed. *You have some serious issues.*

Ignoring his beast, Brad jumped into the slight lull in conversation. "Have you finished eating, Tasha? David should be waiting for us."

She nodded and stood. "I am, if Megan and Justin don't mind cleaning up without me."

Megan made a shooing motion with her hands. "Go, go. I'll give you one free pass. Although next time, I may not be so generous."

Brad rolled his eyes. "You could try being nicer to the first human guest StoneRiver has had in quite some time."

Megan shrugged. "Hey, I hate doing dishes, so sue me."

Tasha snorted. "Try running a bar. It's not as bad as,

say, a restaurant. But there are still plenty of dishes, and sometimes I still do them myself if someone calls in sick."

Andrew asked, "What's a bar?"

Brad jumped in. "Ask your parents."

He dared to put a hand on Tasha's back and barely resisted sucking in a breath. Even through the thin fabric of her shirt—a different one from the night before, which meant she must've borrowed it from his sister—he could feel the heat of her body.

He could only imagine what it would feel like if they were skin to skin.

His dragon hummed. *Yes, yes. We should see what it's like. And then you'd never let her go.*

Not wanting to imagine that, he instead concentrated on Tasha. "Come on."

Gently guiding her toward the front door, he made out Andrew's voice. "I like Tasha. She come back soon?"

As his sister gave a nonanswer, Brad was grateful that human hearing couldn't have picked up Andrew's words.

Because the answer relied on Brad as much as Tasha.

And he was starting to think he should give her more of a chance and see how it went. Provided, of course, Tasha wanted to be kept on StoneRiver.

His dragon murmured, *Then try a little harder to convince her to stay.*

We'll see, dragon. No one can force her to stay on StoneRiver. If she says yes to that, then I won't outright ignore her. But if you think I'm going to start giving flowers and making romantic dinners, then you're clearly crazy.

His beast huffed. *We'll see. I get the feeling someone like*

Tasha wants respect and love instead of empty gestures anyway. Although a few chocolates here and there never hurt anyone.

He mentally grunted to his dragon and concentrated on getting Tasha to David's place as quickly as possible.

Which was easier than he expected since she remained unusually quiet the entire time.

And he had no idea what that meant.

Chapter Four

After months of barely paying attention to Brad, Tasha couldn't stop thinking about how close he sat next to her inside David's office. He was, what, eight inches away from her? And yet he could've been sitting right up against her for all the heat he radiated.

He also smelled good, a mixture of man and pine, almost as if he'd ran through the nearby forest lately and hadn't bothered to change clothes.

She tried to inch to the farthest side of her chair, to help clear her head. Her stupid dreams of him naked and standing over her flashed into her mind. His intense gaze and hungry look making her hot and wet, aching for him in a way she'd never done before.

Damn her dreams for making her realize the drag-onman was sexy.

Not that her attraction was enough to decide her entire life. Still, it made the option of staying on StoneR-iver more appealing.

And it was looking like she would have to stay, at least for the time being. She hadn't thought of any other solution. However, she had one condition to tell David first. So after the pleasantries and him asking her what she'd do, Tasha sat up straighter in her chair and said, "I'm very close to saying yes to staying on StoneRiver. However, I want to talk with Ashley Swift first. It was too late last night and then too early to call this morning, so I haven't had a chance to get some answers from her."

David didn't blink an eye. "I figured as much. She's awake and awaiting your call."

So, it seemed the clan leader was clever, prepared, and automatically thought a few steps ahead.

That made Tasha want to trust him more.

Taking out her cell phone, she eyed first David and then Brad. "Can I have a moment alone?"

The two dragonmen didn't argue and walked to the door. Brad stated, "We'll be right outside," before closing the door behind him.

Taking a deep breath, she dialed the ADDA employee's number. Much as David had said, Ashley answered on the first ring. "Hey, Tasha. I heard what happened. And before I tell you what I think you should do, tell me what you're thinking first."

Ashley had always asked questions and then truly listened to the answers. It was one of the reasons Tasha had finally capitulated and opened her bar's doors to the dragon-shifters. "Apart from mating one of the dragons here, is there any other way I can stay safe and avoid my bar being destroyed?"

"I wish I could snap my fingers and make it all go

away. But I'm afraid David's suggestion is right—staying on StoneRiver is the best thing to do. Especially since I learned how the two men who attacked you were let go with a warning."

What the hell? "How's that possible?"

Ashley sighed. "The League has become smarter, infiltrating local areas of power, ranging from businesses to the police. That's why you need to stay with a dragon clan. At least with ADDA you have me, and a few other trusted employees I know, to help you."

So she really didn't have any other choice but to mate Brad and stay on StoneRiver. And keeping her bar was seeming more like a dream than reality.

In other words, her entire life was about to change dramatically.

Ashley spoke again before Tasha could. "I wish you could come here to PineRock, but it's more believable to ADDA that you've fallen for the part-time security guard than some random guy here. Or, at least it makes it easier for me to sell. They're still being a little iffy when it comes to random human-dragon matings outside of the dragon lottery."

Tasha had never entered the dragon lottery—where, if selected, a man or woman would go on to impregnate or be impregnated by a dragon-shifter—or met someone who had. In fact, she'd never met anyone who'd mated a dragon-shifter until Ashley had mated PineRock's clan leader recently.

In fact, Tasha knew nothing about the dragon equiv-alent of marriage and was tired of being ignorant. Focusing on what her life would probably become, she blurted, "How will I know what to do if I decide to mate Brad? There aren't any other humans here to share their experiences and give advice on how to handle a dragonman."

"Maybe not, but after my own Wes, David is the most understanding dragon leader in the Tahoe area when it comes to humans. If I didn't trust him, I wouldn't suggest for you to live there for a while, let alone promise he would protect you against any League attacks. Ask for his help and he'll give it to you."

Tasha's gut said Ashley spoke the truth. Still, she asked one of her fears, needing to hear the answer. "If I do say yes to this whole thing, will I ever be able to go back to my life? Provided the whole League mess gets figured out eventually, you know better than anyone that there's a taint of sorts attached to humans who associate closely with dragons."

Ashley answered, "I can't guarantee one way or the other that you can go back to the way things used to be. ADDA is trying to avoid the League problem for as long as necessary, which is making things worse in my opinion. But if you don't stay with StoneRiver for at least a short while then I'd say your chances of leading a normal life are about 1 percent."

"That good, huh?" she drawled.

Ashley snorted. "Well, it could be even worse. But in all seriousness, I don't think you have many options, Tasha. If you stay with a dragon clan, then I can see if ADDA will allow you to run your business from StoneR-iver. But that's about all I can do. I don't dangle false hope. And once the League sets its sights on you, your life becomes hell."

While Tasha had suspected everything Ashley had told her, hearing it from her sort-of friend made it all much more real.

Which meant in the end, she had no choice but to stay on StoneRiver and be Brad's mate.

A mixture of emotions rolled through her, mostly contradictory. How could she be disappointed and anticipate the new path? It made no sense.

Maybe because she was starting to see Brad in a new light. Or maybe she looked forward to the new adventure in a mostly foreign place.

Or maybe she just knew that she couldn't change her circumstances and had to make the best of it.

Regardless of the true reasons—she could sort that out later—she replied to Ashley, "Then I'll stay. Just promise me you'll visit soon. I don't know if many of my friends will come and set foot on a dragon clan's land, even if they were allowed."

"So I'm all you've got, huh?" Ashley laughed and then added, "I'll work on it. My mate is a little protective of me since I'm pregnant now, but I can be persuasive."

Tasha probably wouldn't have brought it up by herself, but now that Ashley had mentioned her mate, she dared to ask, "Is it weird being with a dragon-shifter?"

Ashley snorted. "I wish my mate could hear that. But no, it's not weird. Maybe a little different—you have both the human half and the dragon half to contend with. However, they can be wonderful partners. Well, provided you let them know you want an equal footing, which I sense you want as much as me. Dragonmen and women can be rather protective since they treasure family and clan dearly. So just tread carefully in that department and learn to pick your battles."

Would Tasha even know what her battles were? Brad wasn't exactly forthcoming, at least in her experiences to date. "I'll remember that. Just let me know when you can come visit, okay? I think I need to learn more about true mates, mating, and all of that kind of stuff from another human with experience."

Ashley paused. "You know who your true mate is?"

"Yes. I just found out it's Brad."

Ashley clicked her tongue. "No wonder he always stared at you at the bar. Well, the mating will be a fake one—think of it as a kind of green card marriage to stay with the dragons—but it'll be up to you if you want more than that." Ashely paused a beat before asking, "Do you want more?"

Tasha bit her lip and took a second before she answered, "I don't know."

"Then my advice is to figure that out first. If Brad kisses you, it kicks off a mate-claim frenzy. If you don't want it, then they'll have to drug his inner dragon silent and find some place far away to hide you, possibly for years, until his dragon gets over it."

She blinked. "Wait, what? Does he go crazy or something?"

"Sort of. The human half can usually contain the urge to claim their mate for a while, especially if they're as strong as Brad. But inner dragons want their true mates desperately, and even more so after the first kiss.

We can't risk you being near him once you two have kissed."

Just great. Another thing she had to worry about. "On paper, this would all seem really crazy."

Ashley grunted. "Trust me, I know. You're in a new world, Tasha. One you've only dipped your toe into. But call me anytime, and I mean it, if you need answers. Although I'll make sure David assigns one or two people to ease you in and help you understand everything, too. Maybe one of the teachers can help with your transition into clan life and give you classes."

Needing to lighten the mood a little—everything Ashley had revealed was close to overwhelming her—Tasha muttered, "And here I thought I was done with school."

Ashely chuckled. "Considering how even I don't know everything about dragon-shifters despite working with ADDA for so long, there is definitely a lot to learn. But you're smart and quick on your feet—I monitored your bar for months before approaching you with the idea to open it to dragons, remember?—and you'll do just fine. My only order is to ask for help if you need it. This is a new world for you, and no matter how smart or perceptive you are, you'll need some assistance."

That was an understatement if there ever was one. "Oh, I'll call if I need it. Although asking the dragon-shifters will be a little harder."

Ashley replied, "They're a lot like us, and yet different at the same time. Although I would suggest seeing one in their dragon forms soon-ish to help you get used to the idea of dragons flying and landing all around you."

Tasha hadn't thought of that. Dragons weren't allowed to fly over Reno, and she'd only seen a handful in the skies in her entire life. Maybe some people would be scared at seeing a big dragon with its wings spread out behind them, but Tasha was merely curious. Quite a few dragon groupies came to her bar to gawk at the dragonmen and women, and Tasha wondered if their dragon forms was the reason. Well, apart from their hotness, of course. Dragon-shifters tended to win the genetic lottery most of the time. "Okay, I'll ask to see one then. Thanks, Ashley."

"No problem, Tasha. You not only allowed dragon-shifters into your bar, you allowed me and Wes to stay when it would've been easier to kick us out. We'll never forget it."

True, when the League assholes had first tried to force Wes and Ashley to leave, Tasha could've ordered them out. Instead, she'd sent Brad to calm the situation and possibly kick out the League instigators. "It was nothing. You two weren't the ones causing the trouble."

"Still, it means a lot. Although I'm sorry it brought you to this." She paused, some muffled sounds appearing in the background, and then came back on the line. "Apparently I'm late for my self-defense lesson and my mate isn't too happy about it. Still, if you have more questions, let me know. I'll risk his wrath to answer them."

Tasha smiled at the image of Ashley chatting on the phone while her tall mate stood behind her, arms crossed, grumbling about her being tardy. "No, no, that's it for now. I'm sure I'll have tons of them later."

"Okay, then we'll talk again soon. Bye, Tasha."

"Bye."

As she ended the call, Tasha put away her phone and let out a sigh.

All of her years of planning, working hard and saving to open her own place were about to go out the window. If she wanted even a chance at a normal life again, she was going to have to mate a dragon-shifter.

Which meant closing down her bar for the foreseeable future and instead switching her focus to learning everything she could about dragon-shifters.

After a few more seconds to try and calm herself— her life was about to change in a huge way, after all— Tasha stood and went to the door. It was time to tell her future fake husband the news.

Chapter Five

About half an hour later, Brad guided Tasha inside his cottage and into the living room.

Ever since she'd said yes to being his mate, everything had passed by in a blur. David saying he'd get things in line with ADDA, how he'd coordinate Tasha's first lesson with one of the clan teachers, and then David ordering Brad to take the day off to help Tasha adjust and get to know StoneRiver.

With everything going on, he'd barely said more than three sentences to Tasha. But as she sat on the couch and raised her eyebrows at him, he knew they'd finally have a chance to talk alone.

And Brad had no damn idea what to say.

His dragon sighed. *Ask her how's she's doing or if there's anything she wants to know. It's not that hard.*

Tasha's voice prevented Brad from replying to his beast. "The flashing pupils mean your dragon is talking, right? How does that work exactly? No one has explained it as more than dragon-shifters have two personalities inside one head."

He grunted. "Pretty much. The dragon starts to talk to the human half at six or seven years old. Getting along with the inner beast isn't always easy, but if you don't make it work, things can go wrong really fast."

She frowned. "Wrong how?"

His dragon growled. *You're scaring her.*

I doubt it.

Still, Brad sat in the recliner opposite the couch and said, "Well, if an inner dragon goes rogue and takes control, they can cause all kinds of damage. But it's rare to happen, and it'll never happen with me."

The corner of her mouth ticked up. "So sure of that, huh?"

He sat up taller in his chair. "Of course I am. My main job is to protect the clan. A crazy dragon would make that impossible."

She tilted her head, her hair spilling over her shoulder, and it took everything he had not to reach over and brush it back. Because then he might trace her shoulder, the side of her neck, and finally cup her cheek.

And he most assuredly couldn't do that. Tasha showed no sign of wanting more than his protection— arousal didn't equate wanting a future together—and he wasn't going to assume anything.

Which means I'll have to be the one to tell you when she's ready, his dragon stated. *Because you never notice anything about females.*

Not wanting his beast to rehash discussions about their ex—and how his beast had seen the signs that

Amber didn't love them the same way—Brad focused on Tasha. He cleared his throat. "You clearly have more questions. So ask them."

"Is that an order or a request?"

"Does it matter?"

She snorted. "Maybe not in this case. But as long as I'm here, we're to be equals, Brad. This is your clan, but I'm not going to do everything you say just because I'm in the minority here."

He leaned forward and propped his elbows on his thighs. "I'd never order you around, Tasha. Unless we were naked."

Fuck. He hadn't meant to say that, but it seemed his brain and his cock weren't on the same side right now.

To her credit, Tasha didn't frown or instantly admonish him. No, instead she also leaned forward—maybe purposely to show off her cleavage, because he had a clear view—and replied, "If we're ever in that situation, I look forward to it."

He blinked. Had the human really just said that?

His dragon spoke up. *Encourage her.*

How?

Figure it out.

Tasha's gaze roamed down his body and back up again. Every inch she took in sent more blood straight to his cock.

Just what had she talked about with Ashley Swift?

His soon-to-be female spoke again. "Yes, I'm being straightforward. And maybe it'll never happen. But I figure if I'm going to basically marry you for a while, I should be honest. You're attractive, and there's no sense hiding it. If not for the true-mate thing, I might consider the whole acquaintances-with-benefits deal. However, you can't kiss me or it'll start the frenzy. It's best if I test you now, when we're still mostly strangers, so you can shore up your defenses against me."

He frowned. "What the hell are you talking about?"

"You're clearly attracted to me, too, Brad. But if I have children, it'll be with someone I want to spend my life with. A frenzy doesn't guarantee that will happen, so we both need to get used to being around one another without sex happening. And from your dropped jaw, I can see I've surprised you. But honesty will help us in the long run, I think."

At her words, he snapped his jaw closed.

His dragon laughed. *I like her more and more. If she can make you gape, she's worth keeping.*

Ignoring his beast, he focused on the human female sitting across from him. "There's different levels of honesty. But I think it's safe to say that you're the most honest person I've ever met so far."

She grinned. "Good. I kind of like that fact." Her face returned to a more neutral expression, her smile fading far too quickly for his liking. "But I'm serious, Brad. I've agreed to mate you and stay on StoneRiver to avoid being killed. Maybe some women would instantly fall for the hero trying to protect them, but that's not me. If—and that's a big if—this goes anywhere, wonderful. But I want certainty concerning the future, not just some hot sex that fizzles out after a few months."

He growled and blurted, "It would never fizzle. I promise you that."

They both fell silent, staring at one another, and Brad imagined ripping off Tasha's shirt and bra, cupping her breast, and taking her dark peak into his mouth. He could all but feel her nails digging into his scalp as she squirmed.

Brad wanted her. For sex, yes. But if her short, honest conversation was a glimpse of what life would be with her—Tasha always keeping him on his toes—he wanted that, too.

His dragon hummed. *Good, good. Now you have to win her.*

He leaned forward a little more and murmured, "You've laid out a challenge, Natasha Jenkins. One I'm close to accepting."

Her heart rate increased at the same time her pupils widened.

She was thinking of him, much like he'd been thinking of her.

Her voice was husky as she replied, "Well, we'll see how it goes."

"At least that's not an outright no."

"No, it's not."

The temperature in the room kicked up a few more degrees.

Between her heat, her scent, and her beautiful face, Brad was teetering with his control. So it was time to change the subject.

He stood. "Well, there's one way for you to see me naked and not worry about sex."

She raised her brows. "Are you a part-time stripper on the sly or something?"

His lips twitched. "Not on purpose."

"So you just accidentally tear off your clothes in public?"

At the amusement twinkling in her eyes, he itched to pull her close and kiss her.

Not to silence her, but to reward her. It had been far too long since anyone unrelated to him had tried to tease him.

And Brad missed it.

He cleared his throat and put out a hand. "When I'm about to shift into a dragon, yes. Let me show you my dragon form, Tasha. I want to be your first here on StoneRiver."

He half expected her to tease him again, but she stood and slowly placed her hand in his.

As he curled his fingers around hers, electricity raced up his body as their gazes locked again.

Just how in the hell had he ignored and resisted her for all those months?

His dragon huffed. *Good question.*

She murmured, "I'd like that. Although hopefully I can do more than watch. I have no idea what dragon scales feel like, and that's probably a good thing to know about if I'm to live here."

"I'm not sure the texture of dragon scales will come up at the dinner table, but ear scratching might. So I'll have to teach you about that today."

She snorted. "Ear scratching? Like people do with dogs?"

His beast growled. *We are a million times better than a dog.*

He smiled. "Don't compare my dragon to a dog. That's a good first tip, I think."

"Oh, did I insult him? I didn't mean to. I think I still forget there's a second personality listening in to this conversation."

His dragon grunted. *Just wait until I can talk to her. Then she'll meet the better half out of the two.*

Brad replied to Tasha, "Don't worry, he can handle it. And with time, you'll more than remember he's there. Dragon halves can take control sometimes, even when we're in our human forms."

She squeezed his hand. "Then explain it to me as we walk. I'm impatient to see my first ever dragon up close."

His dragon settled down and stood taller inside his mind. *Yes, I want her to see me. So stop wasting time.*

As he walked hand in hand with Tasha out of his house and toward the rear landing area—it was the quieter of the two inside StoneRiver—he did his best to give a basic explanation about inner dragons.

And despite the fact several clan members gave worried looks at Tasha, she never faltered or looked away from anyone who met her gaze.

She was fucking fantastic for so many reasons. And Brad was tired of making up excuses.

From here on out, he would try a little harder at winning his true mate. Maybe, just maybe, things would go better this time around with the right female.

∽

TASHA HAD no problem listening if the speaker had something interesting to say. And for the entire walk to what Brad called the landing area, the dragonman went into detail about his inner dragon.

Oh, she didn't fully understand the part about his dragon "hiding" inside his mind for the first six or so years of his life. But it was fascinating to learn how the dragon half had its own personality, its own opinions, and could even take control of Brad's human form.

She really had barely scratched the surface during her dragon lessons from ADDA, right before she'd opened her bar to the dragon-shifters.

And before she knew it, Brad stopped them inside a giant area surrounded by a tall wall made of carefully stacked rocks. Definitely something built a long time ago, judging by the worn surfaces and various marks on them.

Brad released her hand, and Tasha almost grabbed it again, afraid the spell of normalcy they'd shared during their walk would fade without constant contact. After all, listening to Brad talk about his inner dragon with a mixture of annoyance and fondness had made her more interested in the dragonman by the minute.

However, she was a grown-ass adult and could resist one man. Instead of reaching for him, she tapped her hand against her leg and asked, "So how does this whole shifting thing work? I haven't gotten that lesson yet."

"It's easier if I show you. Of course, to change forms I need to be naked. You can turn around if you want, but then you'll miss the free show."

She blinked. Had Brad just…teased her?

Tasha quickly recovered and decided not to hold

back. She moved her gaze from his face to his broad shoulders, his trim waist, and muscled thighs that she could make out despite his jeans. "Oh, I think I won't be doing that."

She looked at his face again and smiled at his startled expression.

This was clearly a man unused to teasing and humor, at least from a human. But Tasha loved it, and he'd just have to get used to it if he was going to be her mate.

Clearing his throat, Brad turned around and adjusted himself. She snorted. "Oh, dear. Do we need to wait a few minutes or risk giving this show an X-rating?"

He grunted. "Just stand there and I'll get ready. Don't come close to me until I'm in my dragon form and motion for you to approach."

The strain in his voice told her all she needed to know—she was close to pushing him over the edge.

And Tasha didn't want to do that. There was a difference between teasing for fun and going too far to cause anger or distress.

So she watched as he continued to stand with his back to her for about two minutes. Then he took off his shirt, revealing a deliciously wide set of shoulders.

Tasha had always had a thing for shoulders that could make her feel small and protected.

However, she didn't think too much more on it because Brad began to slide down his jeans—slowly, oh so slowly.

It looked like the man was teasing her now.

Since he'd pretty much given her encouragement, Tasha couldn't help herself and whistled. The dragonman glanced over his shoulder with a frown. He growled, "Stop distracting me."

"Sorry, I'll behave. But it's just so much fun to tease you. However, I'm not one of those people who can't take it. So feel free to get back at me at any time."

His pupils flashed between round and slitted before he replied, "Duly noted."

And as he dropped his jeans, revealing no underwear underneath, Tasha bit her bottom lip.

What she wouldn't give to grab his firm ass and dig in her nails.

Brad stepped out of his clothes and she met his gaze again. The dragonman smiled smugly as he slowly turned around.

Curiosity piqued, she looked down south.

And holy hell, the rumor about dragon-shifters being well-endowed was true. Although it seemed he'd taken care of any erection for the time being, which made her wonder just how big he was then.

"Stop staring at my cock and watch me shift," Brad ordered.

Tasha finally tore her gaze away just as Brad glowed ever so slightly. A second later, his arms and legs grew longer, wings slowly emerged from his back, and his nose elongated into a scaled snout.

She had no idea how many seconds passed before a really tall, dark red dragon stood in front of her.

Sure, she'd seen pictures, but nothing compared to the faint sunlight glinting off his scales, turning them a slightly lighter red in places.

For some reason, it made her think of glitter.

Although she suspected Brad wouldn't like that comparison. After all, a glitter dragon didn't exactly sound all that scary or intimidating.

The magnificent beast made a sound in his throat and motioned with a wing for her to come forward.

If it had been an unfamiliar dragon, one that had landed near here randomly, then maybe Tasha would've hesitated. But Brad was agreeing to marry her to protect her, so she went to him without hesitation.

Still, as she approached Brad, she took in his sharp, pointy teeth, the ears standing up from his skull, and even the giant talons of his front paws—hands? Claws? Who knew—resting on the ground. If someone didn't know a dragon-shifter personally, then Tasha could understand how a person might fear a creature like the one in front of her.

Maybe if more people interacted with dragon-shifters, the League members and other anti-dragon assholes would dwindle, making them less of a threat. She filed that under topics to discuss with Ashley at some point in the future.

When she was close enough, Brad lowered his head and gently bumped her shoulder. Taking it as a sign to pet him, she ran her fingers along his snout. The texture was smooth, yet hard and slightly warm. Definitely not the cold, glass-like idea she'd formed from various movies and books.

Brad's dragon hummed and she smiled. "Okay, I was wrong earlier. You're more like a cat. And no, that's not a put down, either. I'd say cute, but I don't think you'd like that, right?"

The dragon grunted and she laughed. "Okay, okay. I'll make up for it with this mysterious ear scratching. Since I didn't get told exactly how to do it, you'll have to give some signs I'm doing it right."

The giant beast took a small step backward and turned his head toward her, putting his ear right in front of her. It was a bit more pointed than a cat's, but the backside was mostly covered in scales. Well, except for a tiny section at the bottom. "Let me guess, scratch you at the bottom, where you can feel it best?"

Another grunt, which she interpreted as a yes. And so Tasha ran her hand down the ear—also firmer than she'd imagined, although it made sense a dragon needed armor-like protection—and finally reached the little area of exposed skin. Brushing her finger there, she felt the heat of the dragon's body. "Well, if I ever get cold, I know what to do now. Have you shift and then I can curl up against the back of your ear. Maybe not the easiest thing to do, but I'm sure we can figure it out."

The dragon huffed in what she thought might be laughter—could a dragon laugh?—and she finally scratched the area with her short nails.

The more she scratched, the more the dragon leaned into the touch and hummed louder.

Yep, definitely more like a cat than a dog.

Just as she was about to ask if she could explore the rest of him, a tall, unknown woman with brown hair and light brown skin ran up to her and Brad. Without preamble, she said, "Shift back, Brad. David needs to see you both ASAP."

Tasha frowned at the urgency in the woman's voice. "What's wrong?"

The younger lady replied, "Let's just say that your mating ceremony needs to happen now or we can't protect you."

She looked into one of Brad's huge dragon eyes but couldn't read his expression. He motioned with his snout for her to stand back and she followed the unknown clan member to the outer perimeter of the landing area.

Since she would be staying on StoneRiver for at least some time, she looked at the younger woman and asked, "You already know my name, but what's yours?"

"I'm Maya Santiago, one of the younger Protectors."

Tasha remembered from her ADDA training earlier in the year that all Protectors in the US spent a year, sometimes two, working with one of the armed forces.

Judging the woman to be in her early twenties, she had to be just out of service.

Tasha asked, "Can you tell me anything about what's going on now? I mean, I was attacked just yesterday so I'm a little worried about what could happen next."

The dragonwoman nodded. "I heard about that, and I'm sorry. A lot of the clan may be wary of humans, but I worked with a lot of them in the Air Force and know not all are bad. But as for what happened, we have some unwanted visitors at the gates. I can't say more than that right now, but if you two don't get mated right away, StoneRiver might not be able to protect you."

She'd been so engrossed in Maya's information that Tasha had missed Brad shifting back into his human form. He stopped right next to them—naked except for his jeans—and stated, "Then let's go. If Tasha's in danger, I need to know everything."

As they walked in some direction she didn't quite know—Tasha really needed a map—she tried to think of what shitstorm had followed her to StoneRiver. Because while she'd mate Brad for his protection, she wanted to help figure out how to tackle both current and future threats, too. It wasn't in her nature to stand back and let others figure stuff out.

However, she needed information before anything else. So somehow Tasha ignored Brad's warm, muscled chest the entire walk to what she discovered was the Protector building from last night.

Chapter Six

Brad clenched his jaw as they walked toward the Protector building, knowing full well that Maya wouldn't give up details she wasn't supposed to.

And yet, he wanted to know what the hell was going on.

His dragon spoke up. *I'm as eager as you are to find out, so walk faster.*

Since his beast's time with Tasha had been cut short, Brad was a little nicer than normal in his reply. *Tasha won't be able to keep up, and I'm not going to carry her without asking.*

Then ask.

No. The building's right up ahead. Now, let me concentrate on getting all the details so we can figure out the best way to protect our mate.

His dragon curled up inside his mind. *At least you're thinking of Tasha as ours. That's a good sign.*

Maybe if he wasn't heading toward a meeting about Tasha's safety, he'd dwell more on the revelation.

But all he knew was that when she'd approached him in dragon form and stroked his scales without thinking or hesitation, it'd shifted something inside him.

He wanted her to approach him like that all the time, making his inner dragon happy. Something about her determination and fascination had made him more curious about the human female.

However, as they entered the building and headed upstairs toward the head Protector's office, Brad pushed aside anything that could distract him.

If he couldn't protect Tasha and keep her on Stone-River, then there would be no chance of a future with her at all.

Maya knocked on the head Protector's door. A few beats later, Jon Bell opened it. His usually smiling face not only had a frown, but irritation also shone in his eyes. Brad didn't wait to ask, "What the hell's going on?"

Jon ignored him and looked at Tasha. "Quickly, I'm Jon Bell, the head of security here. We can get to know each other a little bit better later, but for now, come in."

Brad and Tasha entered the room. The younger dragonwoman who'd escorted them stayed outside and closed the door to give them privacy.

David was there, sitting in the chair in front of Jon's desk. But at their arrival, the clan leader turned around to face them. "We have a situation. Several lawyers and police officers are in one of the meeting rooms here, claiming Tasha is being held on StoneRiver against her will."

Tasha rolled her eyes. "They assume this without actually asking me?"

David bobbed his head. "One of the lawyers is a suspected League sympathizer, so, yes. To him, no human would want to be on a dragon clan voluntarily."

Brad asked, "And the police? Why're they here?"

Jon answered, "They won't tell us until they speak with Tasha. But according to Ashley Swift and a lawyer friend she has, they want to take Tasha away. Something about an old law where no humans are allowed on a dragon's land without express written permission by ADDA. Usually no one bothers if a human is here for a few hours or even a day, but if the League wants her out and vulnerable, they'll use any and every tool in their arsenal."

So much for the League staying away from dragon clans. Apparently, they were getting bolder. Brad suspected there had been some recent changes to their leadership. It was something he'd have to investigate further, only after he could ensure Tasha's safety.

Tasha asked, "So what do we do? Maya mentioned mating Brad ASAP. Will that allow me to stay here?"

David stood and nodded. "Yes, according to Ashley, it will be. She already filed the paperwork this morning before anyone showed up here. And even though it's not approved just yet, she promised it would be. I have no idea how she could guarantee that, but I also didn't ask."

Brad looked at Tasha. Her expression was determined, and maybe a little irritated, but definitely not scared. He asked softly, "Are you okay with that?"

She met his gaze and smiled, the action helping to ease his anger a tiny bit. "I love that you asked me. That's a huge improvement already."

"Tasha," he growled.

She put up a hand. "Sorry, but in tense situations, I sometimes pretend like it's not happening. Teasing helps me." She looked at David, Jon, and back at Brad. "I'm fine with mating Brad right now. However, I can't guarantee I'll go through the whole frenzy thing. I still need time for my new reality to sink in."

Brad grunted. "That's fine."

What he left unsaid was that he planned to win her over anyway, so it wasn't really a concern at all.

His dragon snorted. *You've changed your tune quickly. I like it, though. So I'll help once we deal with the bastards wanting to take away our mate.*

David took something out of his pocket. Opening his fingers, he revealed two simple gold bands. "I had to guess sizes, but they'll work for now."

Seeing the two mating rings made it crystal clear to Brad—he wanted this. It didn't matter if Tasha was human, or if there was no guarantee everything would work out. The rings and ceremony would give him the chance to pursue that future.

And considering Brad had dreaded any thoughts of the future for months, it gave him hope that maybe finding his true mate wasn't such a bad thing after all.

∾

SEEING the two rings lying on David's palm made Tasha even more aware of how similar the dragon-shifters were to humans. They might call it a mating instead of a marriage, but it was basically the same thing.

On top of that, the light glinting off the rings also signaled that her mating was going forward at lightning speed.

Maybe she should be nervous, or wary, or more cautious. But in reality, she looked forward to seeing what could happen with Brad. The time in the landing area had shown her a different side to the dragonman, and not just because of his dragon half. She wanted to know more about him.

Besides liking Brad more, she'd also enjoy giving the middle finger to the lawyers and police officers who wanted to assume what she wanted, or what was best for her.

So she asked David, "Okay, so what do I do now? They didn't give us any sort of mate ceremony training during my previous ADDA sessions."

The corner of David's mouth ticked up. "I doubt it. But in all seriousness, Brad will go first, and you can just mimic him, okay?"

She nodded and turned toward Brad. Before he could say anything, though, she murmured, "I guess shirts and shoes are optional for mating ceremonies?"

Brad smiled. "You liked me naked well enough. So I'm probably overdressed."

She laughed. Tasha enjoyed this new side to Brad. "Well, you just need to be careful not to repeat what happened right before you shifted earlier. We can't have that happening in front of your clan leader and head of security, now, can we?"

Brad's eyes turned heated, and it took everything she had not to let it affect her. Well, at least not too much. Her heart rate jumped up and her clothes suddenly felt too tight.

Thankfully David cleared his throat and stated, "I don't usually rush something this important, but time really is of the essence right now."

Brad picked up one of the rings—the slightly smaller one—and held it out. "Natasha Jenkins, I was hell-bent on staying away from you for months. I let one person's actions affect how I viewed all humans, and you made me realize quickly how wrong I was to do that. Your wit, your beauty, your determination—all make me like you more and more. So I claim you today with the hope of finding out even more about you in the future. Will you accept my mate claim?"

She nodded, and he slipped the ring on the fourth finger of her left hand, the slight weight a reminder of how her life would never be the same.

Brad motioned toward the other ring, and Tasha picked it up. Taking a deep breath, she said what came to mind. "While you were a damn good security guard, I was pretty sure you hated me. It took some extreme circumstances for us to be thrown together, where we had no choice but to learn more about one another. And I think we both were lucky, in a way, that it happened. You're much more than I thought you were, Brad

Harper, and I'm curious to see what else you're made of. So I claim you today with a promise that I'm going to find that out, and whether you like it or not, we're going to have some fun together, too. Do you accept my claim?"

He nodded, his pupils flashing rapidly, and she slowly placed it on his finger. Once done, Brad took her hand and brought it to his lips. The brief brush of his hot, soft lips made her heart skip a beat.

She might not be ready for a full-blown frenzy, but Tasha was more than a little curious about what this dragonman could do when they were alone and naked.

Before her mind could spin any kind of fantasy, David spoke up. "Good, now that's done. I just need you to sign some papers and then I can send the lawyers and police away for the time being."

She somehow forced her gaze from Brad's at those words. "It's that easy?"

David shrugged. "For now. I'm sure they'll be back, but they'll need new charges. It'll give us time to strengthen your defense and plan our strategy for dealing with them."

And so the fight would go on. Later, she'd have to ask Ashley if it ever got any easier being a human tied so closely to a dragon-shifter. Not that Tasha was someone who gave up easily, but it'd be nice to have a goal of some sort of normalcy again one day.

Brad said, "Then let's sign the papers so I can get Tasha home. There's still a lot for her to learn and I don't want to put it off."

She frowned. Of all the things to worry about, her

dragon-shifter education seemed strange at the moment. "Can't we have a small celebration of some sort? Or at least something relaxing to help me recharge before I have to tackle all the obstacles sure to be coming?"

Jon Bell grunted. "She's right, Brad. Give her a little bit of a break. The human hasn't even had a full night's sleep yet."

She smiled at the tall dragonman with black hair and dark brown skin. "I think we're going to get along well, Jon."

He winked at her. "For now. I'm sure you'll hate me later when I check up on you to make sure you're following all the rules."

Brad growled and pulled Tasha to his side. "Watch it, Jon."

She noticed how quickly Brad's pupils flashed. Something was up with his inner beast. She spoke to her dragonman. "Then let's hurry up and sign the papers so we can go, and you can tell me some more about your dragon. Does that work?"

He nodded. "Where are the papers, David?"

"In my office. Come on."

Tasha waved goodbye to Jon and followed the clan leader down the hallway toward his office.

Brad never let her go the entire walk, but she didn't mind.

There was something nice about the warm, solid dragonman at her side.

If only she knew what her future entailed.

For a woman used to planning everything out, the last two days had been a kind of hell for her. And yet, she wasn't angry about it. No, Tasha would just change her plans and learn to enjoy what time she had with Brad.

Maybe they'd work out, maybe they wouldn't, but she wasn't going to give up until she figured out which path they'd go down.

Chapter Seven

The paperwork signing didn't take more than ten minutes. And even with the few extra minutes waiting for David to show proof Tasha was mated to the police, thus giving them no legal reason to stay on Stone-River, it wasn't long before Brad sat on a couch inside his sister's house, Tasha at his side listening to something Andy was saying.

Just as he'd predicted—bringing Tasha to Megan's house gave Brad time to cool his lust and try to focus on how he'd resist his tempting mate when they were finally alone.

His dragon sighed. *I've been restraining myself for months. I would think you could do it for a few hours.*

Brad wanted to believe he could, too. But the mating ceremony had made it all the more real. And combined with the light weight of the ring on his finger, Brad took his duty to protect his female seriously.

Which included shielding her even from himself. He

replied, *Let her get used to everything a little more. Having the children around will help keep us both calm. And fuck knows I need calm if I'm going to convince her to stay on StoneRiver indefinitely.*

So you do want to win her. You'd better get to it.

I'm working on it, he mentally grumbled.

Tasha waved a hand in front of his face and he finally zeroed in on what she said. "Hello, earth to Brad. Are you listening?"

He grunted. "What?"

"Well, despite the return of your grumpiness, Andy suggested we play a game. Are you on board with that?"

Megan jumped in. "While I'm sure it'd be fun, it's already past time for Andy to get ready for bed. I think it's best if you two head home for the night."

His dragon stood up taller inside his mind. *Yes, I like that idea. There's lots we can do without starting a frenzy. Maybe Tasha will be open to some of it.*

As Brad tried to think of an excuse as to why they should stay longer, Tasha stood up. "I could do with some TV time and then head to bed. It's been a long two days, and I'm sure tomorrow will be even longer, if the League has their way."

He spoke to his dragon. *See? She needs rest. No funny business.*

I'm not the one who needed to run to our sister's house. You're the one who's going to have to be careful.

"Brad?" Tasha said with her brows raised. "I get talking with your dragon is a part of who you are, but it really makes conversations super slow at times, doesn't it?"

Megan snorted. "Not for most people. Just my brother."

He shot his sister a dirty look as he stood. "Some of us like to think things through, unlike you, Megan."

"Oh, I think things through. But I don't overanalyze them, like you do."

Tasha placed a hand on his arm, and he stilled, her touch like a welcome rush of warmth against his skin. She murmured, "Come on, Brad. I won't even tease you for the walk back if you want. But I'm being honest here when I say I'm exhausted. Can't we go home?"

At Tasha calling his house home, a longing shot through him. One where she stayed with him forever, and maybe one day gave him a son or daughter, too.

His dragon whispered, *Then be nice to her.*

He took her hand and loved how she instantly curled her fingers around his.

If he wanted more than just lust and sex, he'd just have to work harder at taking care of her, like he was supposed to do as her mate. "Sorry, Tasha. We can go now. I might even have some popcorn we can eat while watching TV or a movie. I probably should find out what type of things my mate likes to watch, for a start."

She grinned. "You may not like all the choices."

"If you're there, I won't care."

Tasha's eyes widened a fraction, but she quickly recovered. "Well, it does seem as if you're full of surprises."

Andy tugged on Tasha's top, and both she and Brad looked down at the young male. He said, "You come for breakfast?"

Tasha replied, "I don't know about breakfast. I'm really tired and want to sleep and sleep. But maybe later tomorrow?"

"Promise?"

"I'll try my best."

Andy nodded. "Okay."

Megan placed her hands on Andy's shoulders and turned him toward the stairs. "All right, mister, it's bath time. Say goodnight."

"G'night."

Megan looked at Tasha. "You have my number, so feel free to call if you need to."

Brad grunted. "I can take care of my mate."

Tasha snorted. "Your mate is standing right here and can speak for herself." She switched her gaze to Meagan. "Thanks. We'll see how the next few days go."

After all the goodbyes were done, Brad took his mate home.

Yes, home was the perfect word. Almost as if the fairly empty house had been waiting for someone so full of life to arrive and fill it.

Tasha was most definitely that person.

And if he had any say in it, she would be his mate forever and not just for a short time to protect her against the League assholes.

Chapter Eight

The next few days flew by in a blur as Tasha tried to catch up on sleep, learn little bits about living with dragon-shifters, and manage her business as best she could from afar.

While she'd told her employees they'd have to close for at least a few days, she'd given them paid vacation time for it. She might not be able to do that indefinitely —and one of them had said they might have to find work elsewhere—but it was a quick fix for the moment.

So as she finished up some paperwork on her laptop, one of the few things Brad and some of the other dragon-shifters had collected from her home, she leaned back and stretched her arms over her head.

Time for a break.

So she went looking for Brad, who had been mostly working from home.

Not that she could really tell what he did all day. The dragonman had been spending more and more time away from her again. Although why he was avoiding her, she didn't fully understand.

From what little she knew about true mates and the needs of an inner dragon, her best guess was because he wanted to protect her from a possible frenzy.

Of course, Ashley had told her that a lot could be done without setting off a mate-claim frenzy, provided the dragon in question was strong enough to avoid kissing their true mate on the lips.

And given how her dreams were filled with one sexy, naked dragon-shifter, she was definitely open to a little fun.

If only she could convince him to do it. He was one of the strongest, most stable men she'd ever met. Surely he was strong enough to keep from starting a frenzy.

Not that she could tell him any of that without talking to him. So it was time to have a frank conversation with Brad before they became unfamiliar with one another again, which she really didn't want.

Tasha finally found him on the back porch, hunched over a computer on the table, typing something. It was almost funny to see the huge dragonman trying to work with such a tiny laptop. "You think they could get you a slightly bigger one. I'm not sure how you can type anything on that thing with your giant hands."

Brad grunted but didn't take his eyes off his screen. "This one is fine. The screens and keyboards in the Protector building are bigger."

She slid across from him and asked, "Then why don't you go and do some work there? I mean, I'm not trying to chase you away or anything, but you said yourself that I'm safe as long as I'm in this house."

He finally met her gaze, his pupils flashing quicker than they usually did. "No fucking way I'm leaving you alone until we're sure the damn League isn't targeting you."

Still being overprotective, as always, it seemed. "I've only gotten one letter addressed to me here, and that was from a lawyer. I wouldn't exactly call it a huge threat." He grunted again and looked back at his laptop. Tasha sighed and added, "What happened to the guy who liked to tease me a little? I haven't seen him in a couple days now, and I miss him."

Clenching the edge of the table, Brad murmured, "Until you decide one way or the other about the frenzy, this is how it has to be. I want to talk with you, hold you, tease you, and so many other things. But my dragon is getting impatient."

Well, then it was time to be blunt and ask some probing questions. "You say he's impatient, but does that mean out of control? If I let you, say, see me naked and touch me, would it help your dragon or make everything worse?

His eyes met hers again, his pupils flashing between round and slitted even quicker than before. "Why would you ask that?"

She leaned forward a little. "Because of two things. One, I like you, Brad, and you're pretty sexy. And two, if it helps your dragon and brings back the man I want to know better, I'm all for it. So it really comes down to whether your dragon can stay grounded or not."

After a few beats, his pupils finally stayed round. "My beast says he can control himself if it means he can feel or taste you."

At his words, heat raced through her body and ended between her thighs.

Maybe, just maybe, she was about to have one of her dream fantasies come to life.

And she was all for it.

Tasha just needed to do like she always did though, and make sure there was a plan in place. "I want to believe you 100 percent, but is there any backup protocol if this goes too far or makes your dragon crazy?"

For the first time in over a day, Brad's lips curled into a faint smile. "You invite me to lick your body from head to toe and still remain practical."

The image of Brad licking down her neck, then to her breast, and finally between her thighs made her squirm a little in her seat. "I never mentioned licking."

"Oh, but I think you want it now."

Damn him, he was right.

Keep it together, Tasha. Just for a little longer. She cleared her throat. "I won't deny it. That'd be pointless anyway, given your superhero-like senses. But I still need to know about any sort of precautions to take. I've been learning more about inner dragons, and sometimes they can lose their heads with a true mate."

His eyes flashed again before he replied, "My dragon says only the weak ones cave. He wouldn't do that. But if you want extra assurances, you can have a phone with David and Jon on speed dial."

As she studied his face, her gut believed him about

staying in control. Although the fact he offered other options only made her want him more.

So now it was just the matter of making it happen.

Standing, she then walked to the sliding door and looked over her shoulder. "Once you're finished, come find me and we'll test your dragon a little, okay?"

And as she went up the stairs and started to undress in her bedroom, Tasha's heart pounded.

She had a feeling this experience would shift her relationship even more with Brad, and yet she was more than a little eager for it to happen. And not just because she wanted to bring the more open version of him back, either.

Ashley kept saying a person's first time with a dragonman was better than anyone could imagine. So it seemed as if Tasha was about to test that theory and see if it were true.

BRAD WAITED until Tasha was gone before he said to his beast, *Are you positive you can do this and not go too far?*

His dragon huffed. *Of course I can. Stop doubting me. Tasting our mate even a little will help. It's one step closer to finally claiming her as our own.*

The words rang with truth. And given how Tasha had basically said they could lick her pussy and make her squirm, Brad was done staying away from her.

He dashed up the stairs and stopped just outside her room. His dragon said, *She should be in our room, not in this one.*

Soon, dragon.

He heard something fall to the floor and his heart rate kicked up.

His mate could be naked, or mostly so, just on the other side of the door.

Blood rushed to his cock at the thought of all her warm, brown skin exposed and ready for his tongue.

Somehow he possessed enough self-control to knock instead of just breaking down the door. Tasha said, "Come in."

Opening the door, he sucked in a breath at a naked Tasha standing in the middle of the floor.

His mouth watered at her hard nipples, the curves of her body, and her long legs.

Legs he wanted around his head as he made her scream his name.

She clicked her tongue. "Are you going to stand there and stare or actually do something to me?"

At the amusement in her voice, his eyes met her gaze again. While there was heat in her eyes, there was also pent-up laughter.

Life would always be interesting with his mate.

Brad walked into the room, shucking his shirt in the process. Her gaze zeroed in on his muscled chest and his cock turned even harder.

What he wouldn't give to have her wrap her fingers around his length and squeeze.

Or to flick her tongue against his head and make him lose his fucking mind.

No. Not yet. He'd please his mate first and prove how much he wanted her. That would bring him one step closer to convincing her to being his and allowing the frenzy.

So Brad kept his jeans on as a sort of barrier. Still, when he reached Tasha, she ran a finger under the waist of them. She murmured, "I've already seen what's under here, so I'm not sure why you're being shy."

"I'm not being shy, love. I'm being practical."

The corner of her mouth ticked up. "You have a naked woman right in front of you and somehow you're being practical."

He cupped her cheek and loved how she leaned into his touch. "If I want more of this, then I have to be."

She searched his gaze, her expression telling him she wanted to say something, but instead, she ran a hand up his chest and down his arm, until she wrapped her fingers around his wrist. She moved his hand to her breast and arched her back into his palm. "Then touch me, Brad. I'm tired of waiting."

His dragon growled. *I can smell how much she wants us. Stop stalling and please her.*

He squeezed her breast before rubbing his palm against her hard nipple. Touching her wasn't enough, though. He needed to find out what her skin tasted like, too. So Brad moved his hand and leaned down, flicking his tongue against her taut peak.

Tasha moaned and he suckled her, loving how she dug her nails into his scalp, letting him know she liked it when he suckled hard, or even lightly bit her.

No soft touches for his mate.

His dragon said, *More, more. Stop making me wait to see how she tastes.*

Soon, dragon. Our mate deserves a little teasing.

As if to make his point, Brad moved to her other breast and continued to slowly suckle, lick, and bite his mate until she was squirming under his lips. She gasped, "How can I be this close already?"

He released her and met her gaze, loving how lost with desire her eyes were. "Because you have the right male with you." He took her shoulders and gently pushed her back toward the bed. "But it's time for me to make you lose your fucking mind. You'd better call my name when you come, Tasha. Do that, and I'll reward you."

Brad waited to see if she'd argue back despite her words a couple days ago, about wanting him to be more dominant in bed.

However, she merely rubbed her hand against his chest and murmured, "That'd better be a promise."

Fuck. His mate grew more perfect by the minute.

His dragon spoke up. *Then stop waiting and act. Lick her pussy and clit till she screams.*

But Brad didn't have to say anything. Tasha sat on the bed, spread her legs, and gently ran a finger through her glistening center.

Damn, she was so fucking wet already.

With a growl, Brad kneeled in front of her and rubbed her thighs. "Remember what I said, Tasha."

Before she could even nod, he moved to her pussy and lightly ran his tongue through her folds. She jumped a little, but then soon spread her legs wider and leaned back on her elbows.

The sight of his mate arching her back as she moved

closer toward his tongue made his cock release a drop of precum.

Since he couldn't fuck her pussy with his cock, he slowly teased her entrance with his tongue instead, moaning at the taste of her sweet honey.

Needing more, he plunged his tongue inside her, loving how her muscles gripped him lightly.

He put his hands under her ass and lifted her even more to his mouth, giving him better access to lick, thrust, and tease her sweet core.

When she was even wetter for him, he pulled back and moved to circle her clit without actually touching it. She buckled her hips and cried out. "More, Brad. Please."

Not wanting to deny his female, he flicked her hard bud with his tongue, soon finding a rhythm that made her moan and squirm more than any other.

And even though his dick was harder than it'd ever been in his life, he focused on his female, both man and beast wanting—no, needing—her to orgasm. Mostly for her, but also for him.

Because it was one of the ways Brad could prove he wanted her as his mate for real.

It didn't take long until Tasha squirmed as she gripped the blanket with her fingers.

Suckling her clit, he lightly nibbled with his teeth, and Tasha cried out before she screamed his name.

Needing to taste her orgasm, Brad moved back to her pussy, lapping at her sweet nectar, groaning at how fucking good she tasted.

When she finally stopped spasming, Brad gave one

last leisurely lick before he kissed each of her thighs and then her lower belly.

So as to not tempt himself, he laid his chin on her abdomen and smiled up at her. Tasha barely raised her head and smiled slowly. "So what's my reward then?"

He gently slapped her hip. "Are you sure you can take more? You look about ready to pass out to me."

She raised her brows. "It'll take more than one orgasm to do that, dragonman. I can take whatever you've got."

His dragon snorted. *She has obviously never been with a dragon-shifter before.*

Good. We'll be her first and last one.

With no argument from his beast, Brad lazily played with Tasha's nipple as he said, "Just be lucky I can't go full force yet. Because in a frenzy, you can't say things like that or my beast will pounce on the opening, interpreting it as a real challenge. You have to set boundaries with inner dragons."

"Oh, if you go too far, I'll say something, trust me. But I'm not a delicate flower who gasps at a few swear words or something. I look forward to your inner dragon later."

His dragon growled. *You had better fucking try to win her over a hell of a lot faster than what you've been doing. I want to claim her.*

He replied to Tasha, "Duly noted. Now, as for your reward…"

And so Brad made his mate come two more times with only his fingers and tongue, loving how he learned exactly what made her orgasm the hardest.

True, his balls were so blue by the end they were probably bordering on purple, but he didn't care.

No female had ever tasted as good, had been as open to his touch, or had ever truly screamed his name so loud.

And with his dragon half somewhat calmed after it all, Brad started to think of how to win Tasha over completely. No more distance or excuses.

In his mind, he'd already claimed her. But to appease his beast, he needed to make it a reality.

Chapter Nine

The next morning, Tasha reached a hand over to the left side of the bed and expected to find the giant, warm hulk of a dragonman.

However, she felt nothing but smooth, cold sheets. Opening her eyes, she saw the empty space and sighed.

She understood why Brad couldn't spend the night with her just yet, but she hadn't expected to feel so disappointed at his absence.

And not just because of his magical tongue, either. She was becoming rather comfortable whenever he was near.

Then she noticed the faint smells of bacon and something she couldn't define, and her stomach rumbled. Maybe Brad was making her breakfast.

Getting up, she quickly dressed and headed down the stairs, eager to see which version of Brad she'd find this morning. If he retreated again, she might just have to give him a swift kick in the ass and tell him to make up his damn mind.

Entering the kitchen, she forgot about her worry at the sight of Brad's bare back, deliciously broad and powerful with defined muscles. Ones that were toned from flying and not from hours a day inside a gym.

But it was the bright yellow apron—complete with three rather impressive ruffles—around his waist that made her smile. "I didn't pin you as a sunny yellow cook who loves flounces."

Grunting, he turned around and shook his head. "My sister gave it to me as a gift when I moved in here. I never thought I'd use it, but I also couldn't throw it away because she always checks up on the gifts she gives me. But since I actually wanted to cook, I figured I'd use it. That way the chances of it getting ruined would go up, and then I could throw away the damn thing with good reason."

She grinned and walked closer toward him, motioning toward the spilled batter on one of the ruffles. "I hope it didn't all end up on you. I'm starving."

His pupils flashed a second before he picked up a plate off the counter and handed it to her.

Looking down, she tried to figure out what it was, apart from the bacon on the side. The big blob was most likely some kind of pancake, but it looked sort of like an amoeba illustration from her middle school days.

Brad sighed. "It's supposed to be a butterfly. I noticed the tattoo on your ankle yesterday and thought you'd like one."

The fact he'd noticed such a detail even though she'd

been naked was impressive. "I do love butterflies. But, hey, as long as the food tastes okay, that's all that matters. You did do a taste test, right?"

He snorted. "I'm not trying to poison you, Tasha. Just eat something before my dragon starts getting huffy."

The thought of his giant red dragon throwing a fit made her laugh. "Okay, okay. There had just better be some coffee, too."

He poured her a mug as she sat at the raised counter overhang. He handed her some silverware at the same time, and Tasha looked at the oddly shaped pancake covered in little things she couldn't identify—fruit or maybe chocolate—and quickly cut a piece. Holding up her fork, she said, "Here goes."

She slid it between her lips and moaned at the springy, slightly sweet taste. The little decorations were blueberries and raisins, apparently, which only made it better.

Brad crossed his arms over his bare chest and raised his brows. "Well? Your moan isn't quite as loud as last night, but I still think it means it's good."

After swallowing her food, she replied, "If your pancake recipe could make me feel as good as an orgasm, then you'd be a millionaire in no time." She winked. "But no, it's not quite that good. Still, I'll have another one for sure." She motioned to the seat next to her. "Join me, Brad. It'll be our first real breakfast together."

And as he served up more food and slid into the chair next to her, the action seemed so simple. But eating breakfast with a man who could tease her, chatting about nothing and everything, was something she'd always wanted.

Maybe she'd stay with Brad for longer than a few weeks.

Of course, she'd need to figure out how to run her business still. Tasha admitted she wasn't far off from wanting a family of her own, but she also loved the challenges and thrills of being her own boss.

She'd just need to figure out how to do it all.

BRAD SPENT the morning working side by side with Tasha in the living room, each of them focusing on their own respective laptops.

To some, it might seem boring or completely ordinary. But to him, it was exactly what he wanted. Because it meant Tasha wanted to spend time with him outside of the bedroom. Breakfast had been the first step, but each bit of encouragement only made his resolve stronger.

His dragon spoke up. *Good. I may be a little better today after last night, but I'm still impatient. I want to claim our mate. So maybe do more than just sit here and stare at a screen.*

We both need to do our work, dragon. Besides, would you want a mate that constantly demanded your attention, no matter what needed to be done? This is just more proof that Tasha is good for us.

His beast grunted. *At least now you're the one trying to convince me of her. Just don't take too long to convince the person that actually matters—Tasha.*

I will, after I finish my duties.

As his dragon curled up to go back to sleep—inner

dragons had little patience for trivial human things like email or typing out reports—Brad lost track of time. However, the doorbell rang and he wondered who it could be.

He stood and motioned for Tasha to stay put. "I don't think anything dangerous could just walk up to my front door but let me make sure."

She nodded. "Although for the future, we need to get me a baseball bat to grab if needed. Just in case you need some help."

The fact his human wanted to be by his side to take on an enemy caused approval to flood his body. "We will. Maybe even later today. However, for now, wait here."

Since Brad didn't have a fancy security system— something he'd fix soon enough—he went to the door and looked through the peephole. On the other side stood the tall, dark-haired form of Ashley Swift. "What is she doing here?" he muttered as he opened the door.

He didn't get to ask a word before the ADDA employee smiled at him and said, "Nice to see you, too, Brad. Where's Tasha?"

He frowned. "Is something wrong?"

"Not technically. But I need to have a little private chat with Tasha about some of the finer details of her staying here."

He studied the human, annoyed that she could be smiling so easily when she clearly had some secrets concerning his mate. "That sounds like something is wrong."

Ashley raised an eyebrow. "You do remember that I'm mated to a dragon clan leader, right? So trying to be all scary and intimidating isn't going to really work, Brad."

He sighed and motioned toward the living room. "She's in there."

"Thank you," Ashley said as she strode right past him.

Apparently, mating a dragon-shifter hadn't changed Ashley's methods at all—stubborn and bold, as always.

His dragon said, *It's good she's acting the same as ever. If she wasn't, then I'd actually be worried.*

After shutting the door, he went to the living room. However, Ashley turned toward him and raised her brows. "I need to talk to her alone. I swear on my unborn child that I'm not going to kidnap her and take her away, Brad. Just let me try to help Tasha."

Okay, that sounded less encouraging than before.

Tasha met his gaze. "It's okay. You mentioned you had some things to do at the Protector building anyway. And I'm sure Ashley can promise to stay with me until you get back."

Ashley nodded. "Of course. I convinced Wes to let me stay all day, so no problem."

His dragon murmured, *She'll be fine. We need to check in with Jon anyway and see if anything has turned up about League activities.*

Brad took one last long look at his mate. "Okay, I'll go. But promise me you'll call my cell phone if you need me."

Tasha smiled. "I will, I promise."

And even though he wanted to stay and protect his mate, Brad knew this was a sort of test. Tasha would sometimes need her own space, and this was his way to prove it to her.

But he couldn't resist going over to brush her cheek and murmur, "I'll see you tonight then."

She placed her hand over his and gently squeezed it. "I look forward to it."

Heat flashed in her eyes and Brad barely suppressed a groan. Resisting his mate was one of the toughest things he'd ever done.

However, after one last caress of her skin, he grunted and exited his own house and headed toward the Protector building. Time to find out if there were any more threats to his mate or not so he could plan for every contingency.

TASHA WAS both relieved and anxious at Ashley's arrival. Even though a friendly face was welcome, the ADDA employee hadn't mentioned she was coming to visit, which probably meant something was up.

So as soon as Brad left, Tasha asked, "What's going on? Just tell me and don't sugarcoat it."

Ashley snorted. "Like I would with you. After all, if you piss off the bartender, who knows what will end up in your drink later. Maybe even a side of spit and coffee grounds?"

In normal times, Tasha would tease Ashley back and maybe banter for a few minutes. But right now, there were more important things to focus on, so she frowned and said, "If I still have a bar to run, after all of this."

Ashley's face became more serious, as evidenced by the firmer line of her lips. "That's part of the reason I'm here, Tasha. No matter what I do, ADDA won't budge on you being able to run your bar from StoneRiver—they're still at a hard no. However, I think I have a compromise that may just work."

Pushing aside the sadness at the first part of Ashley's words—she would deal with the hard truth later—Tasha focused on the latter half. "Which is?"

"First let me stipulate that it requires approval from David Lee first. But provided he agrees to the plan and StoneRiver gives you a tiny piece of their land to build a new place—a bar at the edges of their territory which isn't too far from the town of Truckee or even determined people coming from Reno—then ADDA would allow you to open it and serve both humans and dragon-shifters. I'm sure there could even be a landing area for dragons from other clans, too. It'll be like a kind of experiment for them, to see if it indeed helps bring people together or not since it'd be on dragon-shifter land and ADDA will oversee everything and not local human politicians or governments."

While Tasha would love for nothing more than some of her determined patrons to visit her new bar maybe once in a while or the possibilities for what she could do with a fully integrated bar, Tasha was too rational to jump for joy just yet. "Part of me is excited to try. But what's to keep the same thing from happening with the League all over again? They could just go after my new place."

Ashley nodded. "I've thought of that, trust me. But if

you have both StoneRiver and PineRock on your side, the League may think twice about it. My opinion is that the League idiots grew bolder with their actions over the last few years simply because no new alliances have been formed between the four dragon clans in the greater Tahoe area. But if we get two clans to agree to an alliance, and maybe hint that we want more, it could make the League a bit more cautious. After all, pissing off two clans' worth of dragon-shifters is a little more of a deterrent."

With a dragon alliance to strengthen protections, it could—just maybe—all work out.

The lingering sadness of giving up her business in Reno faded, replaced with a small thrill of anticipation. If Tasha could create her own place—from the design upward—and deliberately plan how to run it so it appealed to both humans and dragon-shifters, she might be able to break new ground. At least locally, since Tasha had no idea how things worked in other parts of the country.

But no such place—bar or otherwise—had been created from the ground up in such a way. ADDA usually recruited existing businesses.

Which made the possibilities endless.

However, she was also practical and needed more information before letting her hopes get too high. "While it all sounds great, you said David has to agree to the plan first. What happens if he doesn't?"

Ashley waved a hand in dismissal. "I suspect he will. Wes thinks David wants to form an alliance with Pine-Rock, so this will make it all happen faster. And before you say I'm too optimistic, there are other possibilities. David has no mate, for example, and maybe wants one. If so, opening up a whole new clan for him to visit and see if he can find his true mate will probably be appealing."

She raised her brows. "You're obviously happy having a mate, but maybe David doesn't want one or isn't ready. I know I hadn't thought of settling down until recently."

Ashley shrugged. "Sometimes it's the unknown that keeps you from wanting to put yourself out there. For you, it was fear of losing control of your business. For my own mate—and myself—it was fear of losing the ability to help dragon-shifters. But you know what? It actually worked out better in the end, and once we saw that, the reservations just melted away. I suspect David is the same. Dragons, in general, want families of their own. So if he's holding back, there's a reason I don't know yet."

Tasha snorted. "And yet, I have a feeling you're going to make it your mission to find out if there is a certain reason for his singlehood."

Ashley grinned. "Of course. I'm a liaison officer now and need to make sure my clan gets along with others."

Tasha nodded. "Then talk with David as soon as you can and let me know his answer. It might make my decision about what to do with Brad a little easier."

Ashley searched her eyes. "Is everything okay?"

She hesitated a second and then decided what the hell. If anyone was going to understand, it would be Ashley. "His dragon is getting impatient. And while Brad is doing everything he can to calm him, I think I have to make a decision about the frenzy pretty soon."

The other woman tilted her head. "And if David says yes to the bar idea, how will it help?"

Relieved she could finally voice some of her thoughts, she answered, "Well, if Brad is supportive, then I'll be more hopeful about a future and probably agree to the frenzy. If Brad tries to forbid me from trying—even though I'll be smart and safe about everything, I'm not an idiot—then I can't imagine a happy future with him. While I do want a family someday, I want more than just being a mom. Otherwise, I'll be miserable."

Ashley took her hand and squeezed. "Well, then we'd better go talk with David ASAP, huh, and get this all figured out?"

"What about Brad? I'm supposed to stay here. And if there wasn't a possible threat to my life, I wouldn't just say yes to being confined. But there is a small chance danger could find me, and I trust his judgment when it comes to my safety."

Ashley shrugged. "I said I wouldn't kidnap you and that I'd stay with you, so I'll be keeping my promise. Besides, we'll be visiting the clan leader, which is one of the safest spots on StoneRiver. And if some League asshole did manage to sneak onto the clan, I have this." The other woman held up what looked like a type of Taser. Ashley continued, "It's for protection, especially since I'm still in the early stages of my self-defense train- ing. All things you'll have to do, too, I'm sure. Maybe we can even start a weekly human meet up. That way we can socialize and appease the dragon halves of our mates at the same time since we'll be doing more than talking—we'll be learning how to defend ourselves."

The thought of being able to talk with other humans mated to dragon-shifters on a regular basis lifted Tasha's doubts a little more about staying on StoneRiver. "I'd love that." Eyeing the Taser, she decided it was good enough for a short walk. So Tasha stood. "Then let's go talk with David. I don't like waiting around for the future, and I can't start planning anything until we have an answer."

Ashley laughed. "I like you more and more, Tasha. I've talked to a lot of humans over the years about dragon-shifters—I helped run the yearly lottery for a while—and most have some fairy-tale type view. But the world needs more practical people. After all, muscles and great sex will only get you so far in life."

And so the pair of them left the cottage and headed for David's office. Tasha didn't complain as she had to almost jog to keep up with the ADDA employee. Her future was so close to changing in a good way, and Tasha was eager to get it all started.

Chapter Ten

Brad had heard about Tasha and Ashley visiting David, but his boss had prevented him from running over and barging into the meeting. Jon had said it was something between David and Tasha, and so Brad had been forced to focus on other things until the end of his workday.

But his day was over, and as he headed home, where he had been assured Tasha had safely returned, it took everything he had not to run toward his house.

Why had she needed to talk with David? Had she made a decision about the frenzy? Or had it been to discuss her business? Something completely unrelated?

Even though he hadn't been mated very long to Tasha, the more time he spent with her, the more he wanted to know about her.

His dragon spoke up. *Stop wondering and walk faster. Why you won't run, I have no idea.*

I'm trying to look casual.

His beast snorted. *Such a human thing to do.*

Brad did pick up his pace a little and, within minutes, was through his front door and calling Tasha's name.

Her reply came from the kitchen, so he strode inside. Tasha sat with Ashley at the counter overhang, the pair of them sipping tea and eating cookies.

Maybe he should be nonchalant, but fuck that. Brad asked, "What did you need to talk to David about?"

Ashley clicked her tongue. "So demanding."

He growled, but Tasha answered before he could say anything. "Be nice to Ashley. She had a proposal and we went to see David about it. And before you growl again, calm down and come closer so we don't have to shout across the kitchen."

As soon as he stood across from the pair, Tasha continued without being prodded. "If I continue to live here, ADDA won't allow me to run my bar in Reno."

A small sense of dread filled his stomach, but Brad managed to keep the feeling hidden deep inside. "So that's what you went to talk to David about?"

She shrugged one shoulder. "In a way. Ashley had a suggestion, one where if David allowed me to build on a small piece of land, I could make a place for humans and dragon-shifters at the edges of StoneRiver's lands. And before you ask, he agreed to it. There are some finer details to work out with regards to the alliance with Pine-Rock, but as soon as I can sell my place in Reno, I can start working on my project here."

He blurted, "So you're going to stay?"

Tasha smiled, the sight making him relax a little.

"That depends. Are you going to say I can't run a bar, even knowing there could be trouble?"

He stared at his mate, taking in her inquisitive brown eyes and the slight tension in her muscles.

Even if he weren't trained to read body language, Brad knew his answer would determine everything.

His beast murmured, *Then don't be a dick about it.*

He replied to Tasha carefully, needing to be honest without scaring her away. "I can't say that I won't ever worry. And I plan to still be a part-time security guard, like before. However, I trust you to be safe about what you do and to listen to what the Protectors and ADDA have to say about safety and precautions. So of course I'm not going to stop you."

She full-on grinned. "I like that answer." But then her brows came together a fraction, and she added, "But you better not change your mind down the road, Brad. Because if we have the frenzy and I'm pregnant, I won't be restricted to the house unless a doctor tells me it's necessary. I'll want to keep working on everything. Can you handle that?"

His dragon half didn't want a pregnant mate anywhere near trouble, even if it was only a small possibility.

And yet, Brad knew he was strong enough to rationalize with his beast and convince him.

His dragon sighed. *I'm not that overprotective.*

You say that now, but you'll get worse once she carries our child.

Maybe. But I wouldn't do anything to drive her away. That much I can promise.

Tasha's voice prevented him from replying. "So? What does Mr. Dragon have to say about it all?"

Not caring that Ashley was there, he moved to the other side of the counter to Tasha's free side and gently cupped her cheek. "He's willing to work on it. But I promise you that I'll make sure he accepts it."

She laid a hand on his chest, and he instantly placed his free hand over hers, not wanting her to move away. He asked, "So? What does this all mean for us?"

Tasha smiled. "I think it means we need to get everything in order so you can finally kiss me on the lips, Mr. Harper."

Relief mixed with anticipation coursed through his body. "So you'll be my mate in all ways then?"

"Yes, as long as you become mine, too. This is an equal standing situation. So you'd better let your dragon know that now."

Ashely snorted and it took everything Brad had not to bark for her leave. The other human said, "Good for you, Tasha. And I think this is my cue to leave. Call me later, okay?"

His mate never moved her gaze from his. "I will."

Ashley left quickly, leaving them alone. Even though he merely cupped Tasha's cheek as she had her hand on his chest, his entire body was on fire for her.

His true mate would truly be his in all ways soon enough.

She murmured, "So what do we need to do before you can kiss me? Now that I've made the decision, I'm sort of impatient to get started."

Her lips were so close, mere inches away, and it took

everything he had not to close the distance to taste her
sweet mouth. "I have to let David and Jon know. Then
it's just a few small things—like setting up regular food
delivery during the frenzy—and then it will be up to you
as to when it finally starts."

She stood and leaned against his body, her hand
lightly stroking his chest. "Then start setting it up now.
Once I make a decision, I don't like to wait. And somehow, I think your dragon is on board with that
approach."

His beast hummed. *Yes, yes. Call everyone right now. Then
we can claim her within the next few hours.*

Brad stroked Tasha's cheek, loving how soft her skin
was. "You're getting pretty good at reading my dragon."

She smiled up at him. "I've been a sort of observer
for years back in Reno. It's helping me tons to figure out
the two sides of you."

His dragon grunted. *Why haven't you called David or Jon
yet? Stop wasting time.*

Give me a second.

I've given you days, so stop dicking around.

Brad sighed out loud and said to Tasha, "I'd better
call Jon and David before my dragon tries to take control.
He will at some point, as you know, but I want the first
time to be mine."

Tasha picked up her cell phone from the counter. Her
voice was husky as she said, "Then call them. I'm almost
as impatient as your dragon."

As she wiggled a little against him, Brad sucked in his
breath as blood rushed to his cock. "Keep doing that and
I won't be able to get anything done."

She laughed. "Okay, okay. Just keep that in your mind as motivation." She stepped back and he nearly pulled her against his body once more. "No more touching until everything's set up. Deal?"

He took his own phone out of his pocket, knowing David and Jon would pick up his number no matter what right now. "Deal. Now, give me a little space to clear my head so I can concentrate."

"I'll do you one better. I'll wait upstairs in your room. I need to make a few quick calls of my own—I already called most of my staff earlier so the bar side of things is taken care of—and get ready for you."

As Tasha walked away, he nearly growled at the sway of her hips.

Soon, real soon, she'd finally be his.

And so Brad went to work, getting everything set up for the duration of the frenzy.

Only once that was done did he go searching for his mate, intent on claiming her as his in all ways.

Chapter Eleven

Tasha did her best not to pace the room as she waited for Brad.

She didn't regret her decision, but it was still a little nerve-racking. After all, being told what it was like to go through a dragon-shifter frenzy would never compare to the real thing.

Still, she had things to help distract her a little as she waited. Even now, when she was mostly naked in only a robe and waiting for a sexy dragonman to claim her, her mind buzzed with ideas about her new business. It would be more than a bar—she wanted a designated eating area, too. And maybe she could hold family events on certain days, outside next to the landing area.

One of her current staff in Reno had even mentioned she wanted to keep working for Tasha. And although she planned to hire some dragons, too, it was a start.

She was so lost in thought about layouts and events

that she jumped slightly when the door finally opened. Brad stood in the doorway in only his jeans, staring at her with his flashing dragon eyes, and she forgot about architecture and menus. Her mate was about to claim her.

She cleared her throat and asked, "Did you finish everything?"

He grunted. "Yes. My shifts are covered, food will arrive, and everyone is aware of what's about to happen."

Even though his sexy gaze made her shiver in a good way, Tasha couldn't help but tease him. "I sure hope that doesn't mean play-by-play summaries going out."

"No. You're mine and only mine, Tasha. I won't share you."

She swallowed at his words, her knees going weak. "And so now what?"

He took a step closer, and then another, her heart thundering with every inch he drew nearer.

By the time Brad stood in front of her, her bathrobe suddenly felt too tight, too confining, too damned in the way.

And then he lightly traced her cheek, down her neck, and then to the neckline of her robe. "Before anything else, I need to make sure you know how this works."

She nodded. "Ashley told me everything, with lots of details. I know your dragon half will come out sometimes and will be focused solely on getting me pregnant."

Brad ran his thumb up to her cheek and then to her lower lip. As he gently brushed it back and forth, Tasha let out a breath. Brad's husky voice said, "Good. Then unless there's any reason for you to object, I'm going to kiss you now."

As her lips throbbed in anticipation, she murmured, "You'd better hurry the hell up then."

The corner of his mouth ticked up a second before he moved his head closer to hers. His hot breath danced against her lips as he said, "As my mate wishes."

And within the next second, his firm, warm lips brushed hers once, twice, and then finally stayed. He nibbled her bottom lip, and she instantly opened her mouth, his tongue sliding inside. Tasha groaned and clung to him as he slowly explored her mouth, licking, tasting, letting her know he wanted her.

One of his hands slid under her robe and cupped her ass. She pressed her hips against his, the hard outline of his cock making her ache for more than a mere kiss.

His hand moved to between her thighs, and she spread them wider, gasping as his finger toyed with her entrance. Brad murmured, "Nice and wet for me. Good. Because my dragon isn't going to hold back much longer."

Because of Brad's wicked fingers, it took everything she had to string together her words. "Then why make me wait? I know dragon halves only focus on the sex part, and I'm fine with that for now."

He slowly slipped a finger inside her, and she gasped. Brad said, "I get the first time, and I'll make damn sure my female is ready."

As he moved in and out of her, Tasha took his lips again, needing to taste him as he made her hotter.

He growled and stroked her tongue as he increased

his pace. Even though Tasha's legs threatened to buckle, she leaned against her mate for support, loving his hardness against her.

Brad finally broke the kiss and removed his finger. She growled in frustration. "Don't you dare stop."

He undid the robe tie at her waist. "Calm down, love. I want us both naked so I can feel your orgasm gripping my dick."

Impatient, Tasha tore off her robe and moved to the bed. "Hurry up, Brad."

His eyes flashed constantly as he shed his jeans and walked toward her, his hard cock jutting from his body.

Tasha may not get the chance during the frenzy, but she licked her lips at the thought of taking him into her mouth and driving him as crazy as he'd done with her the day before.

Brad's voice sounded a little strained as he said, "Fuck, Tasha, I'm not going to last if you keep staring at my dick and licking your sweet lips like that."

She met his gaze and smiled slowly. "Seeing as how if you come inside me I'll orgasm, I'm not all that disappointed." She opened her legs wide and laid her arms above her head. "Claim me, dragonman. I'm ready."

BRAD STILL COULDN'T BELIEVE his beautiful mate lay naked in his bed, waiting for him.

His dragon growled. *Believe it and claim her. She's ours. I want her. If you won't act, then I'll take control.*

Since his inner beast could very well overpower him

in the throes of a mate-claim frenzy, Brad slowly crawled onto the bed until he was on all fours above Tasha. Everything about her was perfect to him—from her expressive eyes to her small breasts to her flaring hips.

And now, he was going to tell her with actions how much he wanted her.

Brad lowered himself onto her body and resisted a hiss as his cock pressed against her warm skin.

Tasha's husky voice reached his ears. "Your mini-dragon isn't close enough yet."

He blinked. "Mini-dragon?"

She grinned. "Your cock."

"Oh no, no. We're not giving nicknames."

She ran a hand down his back and up again, lightly digging her nails into his skin in the process. "The longer you wait, the more I'll try. How about Mr. FireBreather?"

His dragon growled. *Definitely not. Sounds like we have some sort of disease. Don't let her keep going. Fuck her already.*

Ignoring his dragon, Brad ran a hand down Tasha's side and lifted his hips so he could tease her pussy. "I think it's time to make you forget how to talk."

Before she could reply, he took her lips in a quick, rough kiss at the same time he slid a finger inside her.

His mate was so wet and tight, and his cock grew even harder.

It was time to stop taking things slow.

He leaned up, balancing on one arm, and positioned his cock at Tasha's entrance. He met her smoldering gaze, his voice rough to his own ears as he said, "Last chance to turn back."

She arched her hips so that her heat brushed his cock. "No way."

His dragon said, *Hurry, hurry. You're so close. I want her. She needs to carry our young. Fuck her. And then I will, over and over again.*

Brad pressed into Tasha slowly, gritting his teeth with every slow inch. "You're so tight."

"I can take you, Brad. Trust me, the fuller, the better."

No filter for his mate and he loved that about her.

Hell, he loved so many things about her.

And maybe it was too soon, or he should be more cautious given his relationship history, but fuck it. He loved Tasha.

Once the frenzy was over, he'd prove it some more to her before he said it out loud.

His dragon roared. *Stop thinking and start pumping.*

Brad finally filled Tasha to the hilt, took one of her nipples into his mouth, and teased her with his tongue as he moved his hips slowly.

Her nails dug into his scalp, and she moved her own hips faster and faster.

His dragon hummed. *Yes, yes. Give her more. Embrace the dragon side and fuck her quickly.*

Releasing her nipple, Brad met Tasha's gaze and never looked away as he pumped harder, taking care to rub her clit as he went, wanting—no needing—her to come even before he did.

His dragon spoke up. *Don't wait. Don't. She'll come anyway with us. I want my turn. Hurry up.*

Brad ignored his beast, moving his hips fast enough

for the sound of flesh hitting flesh to fill the air. He never stopped playing with Tasha's clit as she gripped his shoulders. Even when she dug her nails in harder, he merely growled and increase his pace.

"Fuck, yes, right there, Brad. So close."

He pressed her hard bud, and Tasha screamed as her pussy milked his cock. The pressure sent Brad over the edge, and with each jet of his semen, Tasha screamed louder.

When they both finally came down, he collapsed on top of Tasha, all while being careful to use his arms to keep from crushing her.

Merely having her warm body next to his while he was still inside her was fucking perfect. There was nowhere else he'd rather be than right here with his mate, the female he loved and wanted to convince to love him back.

His dragon roared. *No more time for thinking, or planning, or human shit. It's my turn. I want our mate.*

Brad managed to get out, "My dragon's coming out," before his beast pushed to the front of his mind and put Brad behind a mental barrier. If he truly needed to break free, he could. But Brad knew his beast needed to claim Tasha as much as the human half did.

So his beast pulled out of Tasha, flipped her onto her stomach, and raised her hips into the air. The slightly deeper voice of his dragon said, "You're mine. I'm going to claim you, over and over, until you know you're mine."

Tasha looked over her shoulder and merely smiled. "No arguments here."

With a roar, his beast plunged into her pussy and

thrust hard. No gentle touches or build up with his dragon. It was just raw desire, lust, and a driving need to fill her until she carried their child.

By the time his dragon came, making Tasha cry out with another orgasm, Brad found his opening and took charge again.

And so it went, day after day, with only minimal breaks, as both man and beast sated their most basic desire to truly claim their mate.

Chapter Twelve

In the weeks after Brad had told Tasha she was finally pregnant—something that was still sinking in—she did her best to learn as much as she could about dragon-shifters so she could fit in on StoneRiver.

Megan and one of the teachers she'd been working with—Brianna—were the people she was closest with on StoneRiver. Ashley came to visit when she could, and Tasha had even met the two non-ADDA-related humans from PineRock who were mated to dragon-shifters, Ryan and Tori.

All in all, she was adjusting. However, today was a special day, and she couldn't help but pace the living room as she waited for Brad to come downstairs.

He finally descended dressed in a suit but no tie, and her mouth fell open.

Yes, he was delicious naked. But something about the fit of the dark suit made him even sexier, if that were possible.

He chuckled. "Don't drool on yourself, love. We don't have time for you to change if we're to be on time for the groundbreaking ceremony."

Right, the ceremony signaling a true beginning to her new life. Well, at least another one added to the dragon-shifter husband and a half-dragon baby on the way.

She closed her mouth and cleared her throat. "Would you rather I pretend I didn't find you irresistible in that outfit?" She gave him one of her heated gazes. "Because it could be nice if you kept it on later and let me peel it away slowly."

His eyes flashed rapidly, and the corner of her mouth ticked up. It was getting easier and easier to provoke his dragon, in a good way of course. Maybe some found the two personalities weird, but she liked how it kept her on her toes.

Tasha walked up to Brad, placed a hand on his chest, and whispered into his ear, "Do you need a moment to tame the beast before we go out?"

He sighed. "Stop calling my dick the beast."

She laughed. "It's too much fun." Leaning back to meet his gaze, she noticed his lips twitching and added, "Besides, you like me teasing you. The quicker you embrace it and stop trying to deny it, the sooner you can up your game for comebacks."

He smiled as he stroked her cheek. "I'm working on it."

"My offer still stands—I can give you a few classes on the subject."

"I'm merely biding my time, Tasha. So when I come out swinging, you'll know."

She grinned at the promise in his words. And as they stared at one another, joy, happiness, and something she'd been trying to hold back rushed through her body.

She'd realized a few days ago that she loved Brad, but she hadn't said the words yet. Partly because she didn't want to ruin the groundbreaking for her new business by having tension between them if he didn't feel the same. But also because she knew he'd been hurt deeply before and she didn't want to appear to rush him.

Brad was the first to move, placing his hand over her lower abdomen, a reminder that a part of him and a part of her was there, growing by the day. He murmured, "And remember, my top priority is protecting you and the baby. Witty remarks won't scare off an enemy. Once things calm down, I can relax a little more."

Tasha sobered a fraction, placing her hand over his and squeezing slightly in reassurance. "You can do both, Brad. Besides, the lawyers have backed off, and it appears the League has as well. I'm tainted goods now, after all. So they'll leave us alone."

She'd learned that once a human woman was pregnant with a dragon-shifter child, the League transferred their efforts to those humans who could still be "saved" and shown the light.

Which was fine with her.

Brad growled. "You're not tainted. You're fucking perfect."

She smiled and placed her free hand on his cheek. "You're so much sweeter than you let on most of the time." He merely grunted, and she couldn't help but give him a quick kiss. "It's okay, you can be sweet with me. I won't tell anyone about the yellow ruffled apron. You can be the big badass to the world."

Brad pulled her against his body and cupped her cheek with one hand. "Your opinion matters the most. I never want to hide from you, Tasha Jenkins. I love you and will fight every day to show you how much I do."

Her heart skipped a beat. Had he really just said that? "You love me?"

He held her even tighter against him. "Yes, I do. And if I need to prove it to you over and over again, until it's undeniable, then I will. You're my mate and my future, Tasha. I love you."

Brad's words were exactly what she needed to hear. "I love you, too, Brad. I know it's been rushed, and even two months ago you barely said two words to me, but so much has changed. We balance each other, I think. And I have never trusted anyone as much as I trust you. The thought of being by your side, raising our child, and watching as we encourage human-dragon relations at our bar and restaurant is simply perfect. I love you."

With a growl, he took her lips in a rough kiss, his tongue sliding between her lips and slowly devouring her mouth. Tasha held onto him tightly, doing her best to kiss him back, the pair of them fighting to show who loved the other more.

Which was perfect and just how their life would be. And Tasha wouldn't have it any other way.

Epilogue

About One Year Later

Brad checked on his napping daughter against his shoulder and was amazed that she was still asleep despite the grand opening.

It was almost as if she knew how important today was for her mom and wasn't going to ruin it.

His dragon snorted. *She is barely three months old. I doubt she worries about more than eating, sleeping, and pooping at this point.*

Just because she can't talk doesn't mean she can't sense things. Any daughter of Tasha's is going to be extraordinary.

He lightly brushed Mia's cheek and smiled. At one point, he never thought he'd be a father, let alone have a mate. And now? He couldn't imagine life without both his females.

And even though dragon-shifter populations skewed male, maybe he'd have another daughter soon, too. He and Tasha had talked about trying for another child once her bar and restaurant was up and running.

His dragon spoke up. *Well, it opens today. Besides, we had that couple month break after the birth and definitely need to make up for it. So maybe we should start practicing a little more, so when we don't need condoms anymore, we can knock it out of the park right away.*

Brad mentally sighed. *That's not how it works, and you know it.*

Still doesn't mean we can't do a little more practicing, just for fun.

Thankfully, Tasha tapped the microphone at the front of the bar area, preventing him from replying to his beast.

Mia moved a little and adjusted her position at her mother's voice, but didn't wake up.

Tasha's voice came over the speakers. "I want to thank everyone for coming today to celebrate the grand opening of the Butterfly Bar and Grill—the butterfly a symbol of change and transformation, which I hope we can do here in some small way. It really has been a joint venture between humans and dragon-shifters to get this place up and running. And in a way, that's perfect because my aim is to help us get to know each other better. Not only humans and dragon-shifters, but also the clan members of both StoneRiver and PineRock. To celebrate this grand opening, we'll have words from both of the clan leaders. So give a warm welcome to our first speaker, David Lee from StoneRiver!"

Applause went up. Brad's gaze went to David, but the dragonman was staring at some human female Brad only vaguely recognized.

His dragon said, *She's the sister of Gabriela Santos's human male.*

That's right—Tiffany Ford. She'd been helping Tasha with the bar and restaurant prep.

Although the longer David stared at the female, the more Brad wondered if she were his true mate.

Jon Bell thumped David on the shoulder, and Stone-River's leader smiled and went up to the stage.

As he gave his welcoming remarks, Tasha snuck to Brad's side. He gave her a quick kiss and murmured, "You did it."

"Of course." She kissed Mia's cheek. "All of this is for her, after all, to give her a better future. I would've fought off tanks to make it happen."

He snorted. "I didn't realize you had superpowers now."

"Of course not, silly. But not for lack of trying."

They grinned at one another, and pure happiness rushed through his body.

Then their daughter squirmed a little, and they both stared at her as she settled back down. Wrapping his free arm around his mate's waist, Brad took a second to memorize the moment. After all, he stood inside a place signaling possible change for the two most important people in his life. Sure, it was only the beginning. But with Tasha and Mia at his side, he would do whatever it took to protect the people he loved.

Author's Note

I hope you enjoyed Brad and Tasha's story! It took us to another clan near Tahoe and begins the first of three books set on StoneRiver.

I hinted at the next book in the epilogue—it'll be about StoneRiver's leader David Lee and Tiffany Ford (Ryan's little sister). I had originally planned to release this in January 2021, but I overbooked myself this year and had to push it back. I will release *The Dragon's Weakness* in 2021, but I'm still deciding the exact date. (I've written a lot of dragon-shifters in 2020, so I'm taking a one book break with my sci-fi romance series before diving back into them again!) You can always keep up-to-date with release news on my website or with my newsletter.

And now I have some people to thank for getting this out into the world:

- To Becky Johnson and her team at Hot Tree Editing. They always do a fantastic job.
- To all my beta readers—Sabrina D., Sandy H., and Iliana G., you do an amazing job at finding those lingering typos and minor inconsistencies.

And as always, a huge thank you to you, the reader, for either enjoying my dragons for the first time, or for following me from my longer books to this series. Writing is the best job in the world and it's your support that makes it so I can keep doing it.

Until next time, happy reading!

PS—To keep up-to-date with new releases and other goodies, please join my newsletter at www.JessieDonovan.com

The Conquest

KELDERAN RUNIC WARRIORS #1

Leader of a human colony planet, Taryn Demara has much more on her plate than maintaining peace or ensuring her people have enough to eat. Due to a virus that affects male embryos in the womb, there is a shortage of men. For decades, her people have enticed ships to their planet and tricked the men into staying. However, a ship hasn't been spotted in eight years. So when the blip finally shows on the radar, Taryn is determined to conquer the newcomers at any cost to ensure her people's survival.

Prince Kason tro el Vallen needs to find a suitable planet for his people to colonize. The Kelderans are running out of options despite the fact one is staring them in the face —Planet Jasvar. Because a group of Kelderan scientists disappeared there a decade ago never to return, his people dismiss the planet as cursed. But Kason doesn't believe in curses and takes on the mission to explore the planet to prove it. As his ship approaches Jasvar, a distress signal chimes in and Kason takes a group down to the planet's surface to explore. What he didn't expect was for a band of females to try and capture him.

As Taryn and Kason measure up and try to outsmart each other, they soon realize they've found their match. The only question is whether they ignore the spark between them and focus on their respective people's survival or can they find a path where they both succeed?

The Conquest is available in paperback.

Also by Jessie Donovan

Asylums for Magical Threats

Blaze of Secrets (AMT #1)

Frozen Desires (AMT #2)

Shadow of Temptation (AMT #3)

Flare of Promise (AMT #4)

Cascade Shifters

Convincing the Cougar (CS #0.5)

Reclaiming the Wolf (CS #1)

Cougar's First Christmas (CS #2)

Resisting the Cougar (CS #3)

Kelderan Runic Warriors

The Conquest (KRW #1)

The Barren (KRW #2)

The Heir (KRW #3)

The Forbidden (KRW #4)

The Hidden (KRW #5)

The Survivor / Kajala Mayven (KRW #6 / 2021)

Lochguard Highland Dragons

The Dragon's Dilemma (LHD #1)

The Dragon Guardian (LHD #2)

The Dragon's Heart (LHD #3)

The Dragon Warrior (LHD #4)

The Dragon Family (LHD #5)

The Dragon's Discovery (LHD #6)

The Dragon's Pursuit (LHD #7)

The Dragon Collective / Cat & Lachlan (LHD #8 / May 2021)

Love in Scotland

Crazy Scottish Love (LiS #1)

Chaotic Scottish Wedding (LiS #2)

Stonefire Dragons

Sacrificed to the Dragon (SD #1)

Seducing the Dragon (SD #2)

Revealing the Dragons (SD #3)

Healed by the Dragon (SD #4)

Reawakening the Dragon (SD #5)

Loved by the Dragon (SD #6)

Surrendering to the Dragon (SD #7)

Cured by the Dragon (SD #8)

Aiding the Dragon (SD #9)

Finding the Dragon (SD #10)

Craved by the Dragon (SD #11)

Persuading the Dragon (SD #12)

Treasured by the Dragon (SD #13)

Captivating the Dragon / Hayley & Nathan (SD #14, TBD)

Stonefire Dragons Shorts

Meeting the Humans (SDS #1)

The Dragon Camp (SDS #2)

The Dragon Play (SDS #3)

Stonefire Dragons Universe

Winning Skyhunter (SDU #1)

Transforming Snowridge (SDU #2)

Tahoe Dragon Mates

The Dragon's Choice (TDM #1)

The Dragon's Need (TDM #2)

The Dragon's Bidder (TDM #3)

The Dragon's Charge (TDM #4)

The Dragon's Weakness / David & Tiffany (TDM #5 / 2021)

WRITING AS LIZZIE ENGLAND

Her Fantasy

Holt: The CEO

Callan: The Highlander

Adam: The Duke

Gabe: The Rock Star

About the Author

Jessie Donovan has sold over half a million books, has given away hundreds of thousands more to readers for free, and has even hit the *NY Times* and *USA Today* bestseller lists. She is best known for her dragon-shifter series, but also writes about elemental magic users, alien warriors, and even has a crazy romantic comedy series set in Scotland. When not reading a book, attempting to tame her yard, or traipsing around some foreign country on a shoestring, she can often be found interacting with her readers on Facebook. She lives near Seattle, where, yes, it rains a lot but it also makes everything green.

Visit her website at: www.JessieDonovan.com

Printed in Great Britain
by Amazon